NEW YORK REVIEW BO
CLASSICS

SUN CITY

TOVE JANSSON (1914–2001) was born in Helsinki into
Finland's Swedish-speaking minority. Her father was a sculptor
and her mother a graphic designer and illustrator. Winters were
spent in the family's art-filled studio and summers in a fisher-
man's cottage in the Pellinge archipelago, a setting that would
later figure in Jansson's writing for adults and children. Jansson
loved books as a child and set out from an early age to be an
artist. Her first illustration was published when she was fifteen
years old; four years later a picture book appeared under a
pseudonym. After attending art schools in both Stockholm and
Paris, she returned to Helsinki, where in the 1940s and '50s she
won acclaim for her paintings and murals. From 1929 until 1953
Jansson drew humorous illustrations and political cartoons for
the left-leaning anti-Fascist Finnish-Swedish magazine *Garm*,
and it was there that what was to become Jansson's most
famous creation, Moomintroll, a hippopotamus-like character
with a dreamy disposition, made his first appearance. Jansson
went on to write about the adventures of Moomintroll, the
Moomin family, and their curious friends in a long-running
comic strip and in a series of books for children that have been
translated throughout the world, inspiring films, several
television series, an opera, and theme parks in Finland and
Japan. Jansson also wrote eleven novels and short-story
collections for adults, including *The Summer Book*, *The True
Deceiver*, *The Woman Who Borrowed Memories*, and *Fair Play*

(available as NYRB Classics). In 1994 she was awarded the Prize of the Swedish Academy. Jansson and her companion, the artist Tuulikki Pietilä, continued to live part time in a cottage on the remote outer edge of Pellinge until 1991.

THOMAS TEAL has translated many of Tove Jansson's works into English, beginning in the 1970s with *The Summer Book* and *Sun City* and more recently, *The True Deceiver* (2009, winner of the Best Translated Book Award), *Fair Play* (2011, winner of the Bernard Shaw Prize for translation from the Swedish), and, with Silvester Mazzarella, *The Woman Who Borrowed Memories* (2014). He lives in Massachusetts.

TOVE JANSSON IN NEW YORK REVIEW BOOKS

Fair Play
Translated by Thomas Teal
Introduction by Ali Smith

The Summer Book
Translated by Thomas Teal
Introduction by Kathryn Davis

Sun City
Translated by Thomas Teal

The True Deceiver
Translated by Thomas Teal
Introduction by Ali Smith

The Woman Who Borrowed Memories: Selected Stories
Translated by Thomas Teal and Silvester Mazzarella
Introduction by Lauren Groff

Alice's Adventures in Wonderland
By Lewis Carroll
Illustrated by Tove Jansson

SUN CITY

TOVE JANSSON

Translated from the Swedish by
THOMAS TEAL

NEW YORK REVIEW BOOKS

nyrb

New York

THIS IS A NEW YORK REVIEW BOOK
PUBLISHED BY THE NEW YORK REVIEW OF BOOKS
207 East 32nd Street, New York, NY 10016
www.nyrb.com

First published as a New York Review Books Classic in 2025.
Published in the Swedish language as *Solstaden*.

Library of Congress Cataloging-in-Publication Data
Names: Jansson, Tove, author. | Teal, Thomas, translator.
Title: Sun city / by Tove Jansson ; translated from the Swedish by Thomas Teal.
Other titles: Solstaden. English
Description: New York : New York Review Books, 2024. | Series: New York
  Review Books classics
Identifiers: LCCN 2024009642 (print) | LCCN 2024009643 (ebook) | ISBN
  9781681378657 (paperback) | ISBN 9781681378664 (ebook)
Subjects: LCGFT: Novels.
Classification: LCC PT9875.J37 S5813 2024 (print) | LCC PT9875.J37 (ebook)
  | DDC 839.73/74—dc23/eng/20240304
LC record available at https://lccn.loc.gov/2024009642
LC ebook record available at https://lccn.loc.gov/2024009643

ISBN 978-1-68137-865-7
Available as an electronic book; ISBN 978-1-68137-866-4

Printed in the United States of America on acid-free paper.
10 9 8 7 6 5 4 3 2 1

I traveled through America, through Florida, and came one night to a city that was completely silent. The next morning it was just as quiet and empty. The open porches rested in their greenery with long rows of rocking chairs, all turned to the street. The stillness was almost awful. And then I understood the city was one of the sun cities, the cities of the elderly where sun is guaranteed year-round. Everything is set up for rest and senescence, inexorable and ideal.

I have called the city St. Petersburg but it could just as well have another name. And calm it is not; it's just as cool and adventurous a place as every place else on Earth. I have tried to write a book about becoming old. And described the love between two very young and beautiful people who live in the city of the elderly.

In America, and very intensely in Florida, a new belief that Jesus is returning, now, in the end times, is widespread, and it is the youth that are awaiting His return. I have made Bounty Joe one of those awaiting this. He works security on the movie-ship, the mutiny-ship *Bounty*, which sits anchored out in St. Petersburg's harbor.

The whole city, as I experienced it, is a sort of last beach for departure and arrival, an open possibility headed anywhere. The sun city is a lovable, horrible, and very alive city.

—TOVE JANSSON
Translated from the Swedish by Maya Weeks

"SUN CITIES,

wonderful, peaceful towns, where
we guarantee perpetual sunshine,
paradise on earth, as refreshing
as old wine . . ."

—from a brochure

1 In St. Petersburg, Florida, where the weather is always warm and esplanades of palm trees skirt the blue sea, the streets are straight and broad and the houses are surrounded by luxuriant trees and bushes. In the fancy, placid neighborhoods the houses are mostly wooden and often white, and they have open verandas where rocking chairs stand outdoors all year, close beside one another in long rows. It is very quiet in the mornings, and the streets lie empty in their perpetual sunshine. By and by the guests come out on the verandas and down the steps and walk slowly over to the Garden or some other nice cafeteria. They often go in small groups or two by two. Later in the morning they sit in their rocking chairs or go for a little walk.

There are more hairdressers in St. Petersburg than anywhere else in the country, and they are specialists at creating airy little puffs of thin white hair. Hundreds of old ladies stroll beneath the palm trees with white curls covering their heads. There are fewer gentlemen, however. In the guesthouses, they all have their own rooms, or they share with another person—some of them for only a short time in the even, healthful climate, but most of them for as long as they have left. No one is sick, that is, not in the normal sense of sick in bed. Such matters are attended to incredibly swiftly by ambulances that never sound their sirens. There are lots of squirrels in the trees, not to mention the birds, and all these animals are tame to the point of impudence. A lot of stores carry hearing aids and other therapeutic devices. Signs in clear, bright colors announce immediate blood pressure checks on every block and offer all sorts of information about such things as pensions, cremation, and legal problems. In addition, the shops have put a lot of thought into offering a wide selection of knitting patterns, yarns, games, crafts materials, and the like, and their customers can be sure of a friendly and helpful reception. Those who wander down the avenue toward the bay or up toward the City Park and the church meet no children and no hippies and no dogs. Only on the weekends are the pier and the bay front filled with people, who have come to this attractive city to look at the movie ship, *Bounty*. Then the beaches are lively and colorful, and only at dusk do the last cars drive away.

The Berkeley Arms was located three blocks up Second Avenue. It was two stories high, and from the corner room on the second floor could be seen a bit of the

ocean and the *Bounty*'s rigging, which was illuminated
at night. The veranda at the Berkeley Arms was prettier
than most, graced with a carved wooden railing. The
fact that there were only eight rocking chairs gave it an
intimate and friendly appearance. It might be added
that the house was very old, almost seventy-five years.

Twice a day, Bounty Joe drove down the avenue on
his motorcycle—a little before eleven when the ticket
booth opened, and again in the evening when the rigging was lit. He drove at a terrific speed with the throt-
tle wide open, and at the curve by the corner where
Palmer's was he would stick out one leg and let the sole
of his boot skim the asphalt. Then it was quiet again.
Bounty Joe was in love with Linda, who did the clean-
ing at the Berkeley Arms.

Mrs. Elizabeth Morris of Grand Island, Nebraska,
seventy-seven years old, had the second rocking chair
from the railing by the big magnolia. Next to the magnolia was Mr. Thompson, who pretended to be deaf,
and on the other side was Miss Peabody, who was very
shy. So Mrs. Morris could sit and think in peace. She
had come to St. Petersburg several weeks earlier, alone,
with a sore throat, and once at the Berkeley Arms her
voice disappeared completely. On a page from her notebook Mrs. Morris had supplied information about her
name, her condition, and some antique furniture that
was to arrive later. Silence protected her from the reck-
less need to confide in other people that can be so dangerous at the end of a long, lonely journey. When her
voice returned, the hazardous period of confidential fer-

vor had passed. The others had grown used to her silence and did not ask questions.

Elizabeth Morris was solidly built, with an unusually erect posture. The only make-up she used was applied to her eyebrows, which grew in carefully outlined, powerful, dark blue wings below her gray hair and gave her a distinctly inquisitive appearance. But it was very seldom that anyone saw her eyes.

Miss Peabody leaned forward. "You have so many different sunglasses," she said.

"Three," Mrs. Morris said. "I can make the street blue or brown or pink. The blue one is the best."

Bounty Joe drove by on his motorcycle. He accelerated after the curve and roared off in a straight line toward the bay. On the back of his bike he had painted a big white cross.

"He farts worse than I do," said Mr. Thompson.

They waited for the mail. Every morning Miss Frey came out on the veranda with the mail. Sometimes she wore green slacks and sometimes pink. A skinny old lizard of sixty-five in pink slacks. Women! thought Thompson. He made himself stiff as a post in his chair and gave a long, howling groan from the corner of his mouth.

Peabody grabbed hold of Mrs. Morris's arm and screamed, "An attack, it's an attack, do something!" and Elizabeth Morris jerked away as if she had been bitten. Farther down the veranda Mrs. Rubinstein remarked that Thompson's performance, if it was supposed to be a dress rehearsal, had not been very successful. Miss Peabody gave Mrs. Morris a sidelong look and whispered an apology. She had small, narrow front teeth and very much resembled a mouse. Mrs. Morris would have to understand that that's the way she always was, much too impulsive, much too easily taken in—it wasn't her fault . . .

The morning was cool and fresh and smelled of grass. The smell of grass is the same wherever a lawn is mowed. I shouldn't have pulled away, Elizabeth Morris thought. It happens every time someone touches me, and now I've hurt the feelings of this mouse.

The rocking chairs were too close together. Only Hannah Higgins was actually rocking. She was always rocking, slowly and peacefully back and forth. She had her scissors and pen and a polystyrene egg carton, and she was very deftly cutting out lilies with deep cups and four outspread petals, one after the other. These lilies always stood on the piano at Easter. At Christmas, Mrs. Higgins cut out snowflakes and Christmas stars. It was remarkable how many things could be made from egg cartons. Her nearsighted eyes followed the movements of the scissors very carefully from behind thick glasses. Her broad face was covered with thousands of microscopic wrinkles, as tiny as the wrinkles in crepe paper. She would be seventy-eight in June. Mrs. Morris had noticed that it took a certain amount of attention to keep a rocking chair from rocking. The least motion would set it going. She learned quickly, but every time she arose from the blessed chair her legs were stiff from suppressed tension. Sometimes she wondered if it was the same for the others.

When Miss Frey came out of the vestibule she said,

"Hi everybody, sunshine again." She said this every morning, but today she was tired and said it more sharply than usual. Thoughtlessly, as if she were guided by demons, she made straight for Mrs. Rubinstein. She walked right up to her and in that tone of voice occasionally used for very small dogs or other people's children, she said, "A little letter! A little letter in the mail!" The huge, black-eyed woman turned slowly in her chair and looked at Miss Frey, at the worn, painted face beneath the wig, and then she lowered her eyes just as slowly and stared at the letter, without taking it. They all knew that now she was going to be obscene again. Miss Frey's hand began to tremble, and finally Mrs. Rubinstein spoke. "My dear Miss Frey," she said, with caustic charm. "My own little letter with its own little stamps. Modesty, Miss Frey, only modesty keeps me from telling you what to do with this letter." And she gave a short, hoarse laugh that indicated clearly where Miss Frey could dispose of the letter. Thompson sat up in his chair. "What did she say?" he said. "Did she say something obscene again?"

"Nothing important," Mrs. Morris said.

Miss Frey blushed. She gave Mrs. Rubinstein a playful pat on the shoulder and said, "Oh my, how wicked we can be," dropped the letter on the floor, and walked away.

"What did she say?" Thompson asked again.

Through Mrs. Morris's sunglasses the lawn was blue, the emptiness of the street was like a distant moonscape, and Thompson looked blue and sickly. "Nothing important," she said soothingly. "Mrs. Rubinstein was trying to be funny."

"But what did she say? What did she say?" Thompson insisted. He got up from his chair and pushed his crooked little features right in her face and screamed that that was the way it always was with women! "A person never gets to hear anything funny! A person might as well be dead! Dead as a doornail! And that goes for you too, whatever your name is!" He stood there waiting with his hand behind his ear, and the whole veranda was absolutely silent. Mrs. Morris took off her glasses and when the man wasn't blue any more he looked comparatively normal. She replied coolly that what Mrs. Rubinstein had meant presumably was that Miss Frey could use the letter in question for toilet paper. Thompson listened carefully and then sat back down in his rocking chair. "Very funny," he said, and turned his gaze out toward the street. "Ladies, you are irresistibly hilarious."

It was possible that the strictly frontal placement of the rocking chairs, parallel to each other and facing straight ahead, was the only practicable arrangement. It is probably difficult, thought Mrs. Morris, to place rocking chairs in groups, that is, rocking toward each other. It would take a great deal of space, and in the long run it might be tiresome. Of course the original, the natural idea was a single rocking chair in motion in an otherwise static room.

"I have to go," said Miss Peabody. "I have some things to wash out in my room." She began to sob, and left the veranda hurriedly. Mrs. Higgins observed that now she was all upset again, poor little thing, and Mrs. Rubinstein lit another cigarette and replied that all Peabodies in all ages have always rushed up to their rooms whenever they got upset. They were always so compassionate, and they always had to be comforted all the time. She opened her paper and read about the world, knowingly and contemptuously. It was her fourth cigarette before lunch. Rebecca Rubinstein was eighty-one years old. Her hair was a white tiara, and below her half-closed eyelids her cheeks hung in smooth heavy folds, still with the full color of slightly overripe fruit.

Dead as a doornail, thought Elizabeth Morris, pretending to sleep behind her glasses. That was his trump card. It wasn't playing fair, but the old bastard had to have his fun. I don't believe, she thought seriously, I don't believe there are so many things left to be afraid of. Nebraska, maybe, and confidences, and certain kinds of music, but not death. Not death, that isn't important, and making an impression on people, that isn't important either, not any more. She forget to mention fear of her room—the room you leave open behind you can be full of pitiful carelessness. You have to hide away the signs and appurtenances of old age, small unesthetic oversights, all the supporting constructions of helplessness, so unnoticed and so obvious. Mrs. Morris hid things, she tried to restore the dignity of objects, and every day she did her best to present Linda with an empty and impersonal room. By the time she had dressed and hidden things, she was tired, but she never dared fall asleep on the veranda. She might snore, her mouth might fall open. Linda's vacuum cleaner droned back and forth in the vestibule. Sometimes it hit the wall and then continued on again. Mrs. Morris fell calmly asleep. Her head sank to one side and she slept silently, her teeth firmly closed. The Pihalga sisters stood up simultaneously at the other end of the veranda. They took their books and wandered slowly down toward the bay. When they were reading, the Pihalga sisters were completely cut off from everything that happened around them. And they were almost always reading.

As Evelyn Peabody went up the stairs, one step at a time, she carried with her a great compassion that only swelled and grew heavier and more unwieldy every time she did not dare to defend what she believed. Word by word and step by step she went over the disgraceful and unnecessary conversation on the veranda. Oh these people who threw words around the way you threw stones or tossed out garbage! And poor old Mr. Thompson, who was left out of everything! Saying he might just as well be dead. And she had run away and told another fib. She didn't have any clothes to wash out. How did it happen that a person who loved the truth had to tell so many fibs and that a person who sought justice should have such a hard time fighting? Imagine saying that he might just as well be dead! How dreadful! But he was so right, a man of eighty has survived a good deal longer than he ought. She was seventy-four, absolutely nothing for a woman. He was poor too, and lived on the charity of the house and by all appearances had been a good-for-nothing all his life. That was what happened when you didn't plan ahead!

Miss Peabody decided to be nice to him and show him as much understanding as she could, in spite of his being such a dreadful, cross old man. She rinsed out a scarf for the sake of truth and got out her long gray dress and began to take it in. A person shrank as the years went by. And it was soothing to sew. Evelyn Peabody had been sewing all her life, altering old clothes and turning and taking in and letting out. It took skill and patience to hide what was worn and poorly made and to emphasize what was pretty. Later, at the Salon, the fabrics were new, but the art of hiding and emphasizing was still essential. She sewed swiftly and surely. Nowadays her eyes only lasted half an hour at a time. Miss Peabody never sewed for anyone but herself any more. As the needle flew through the fabric taking a long row of small, even bites, she always thought about the ladies who wanted sweat pads under the arms, the ladies who never recognized her because they only looked in the mirror, and when she was through with them she thought about the dreamlike morning when Evelyn Peabody won the State Lottery. No one did any work that morning. Miss Arundell screamed, "Dear God, *her* of all people! Look at her, she's pale with joy . . . " They asked her what she was going to buy and she cried, "Sunshine! Sunshine! A room of my very own!" That was what she had answered, without having to think about it for an instant. Her body was small and cold and she had won on her own, with her own lottery ticket, and finally there was justice.

When Linda came in with clean towels, Miss Peabody stood up. She always stood up when Linda came into her room. It was a ritual. She was captivated every time by the same calm, dazzling smile that was so unbelievably beautiful, and she smiled back with her hand in front of her mouth. Linda walked unhurriedly into the bathroom. She was always dressed in black, and her black hair hung down her back in a sparkling shock. Her well-formed face was pale, with light shadows of sadness that lay completely at rest. Linda was a Mexican name meaning sweet and lovable.

On the veranda, Hannah Higgins continued cutting at the egg carton, which she held right in front of her nose, adding lily after lily to the collection in her lap. She mentioned that there were no yellow pipe cleaners this year, so the pistils would have to be green. Out of habit, Mrs. Rubinstein wondered if she ought to say something obscene about pistils, but she lost the impulse and let her heavy eyelids sink over her immense disdain. She disdained Easter decorations, verandas, pleasant climates, and, for that matter, everything that conveniently could be disdained on a pretty, empty day in St. Petersburg, Florida. Thompson slept. And now, said Mrs. Higgins, now it was almost time for the Spring Ball, and for her part she was planning to go in black. It was a good color for old women, at least where she came from, and especially if you're overweight. Suddenly she dropped what was in her hands, threw her head back, and laughed—a surprisingly clear almost innocent laugh. Thompson would make a fine escort—one of them couldn't see and the other couldn't hear! Wasn't that funny? Mrs. Rubinstein listened distractedly. She looked at her attractive old hands and the rings that adorned them. Abrascha's ring was the largest. In spite of its vulgarity, she wore it always. His monthly letter was four days late. Egg cartons. Easter lilies. A farmer's wife in black. She turned her large face with its prominent nose toward the street and Friendship's Rest that lay opposite. They had come back from breakfast and all the rocking chairs were occupied. A dozen white faces staring straight ahead, a dozen old asses, each in its own rocking chair, thought Mrs. Rubinstein. And soon they'll be swinging them around as best they can at the Senior Club's Spring Ball. *Goyim nakhes*, she added in silent contempt, which in translation means "Gentile joys."

Miss Peabody stood waiting behind a palm tree. A little before twelve, Thompson usually went around the corner to Palmer's and had a beer. It was said that he did this to show his disdain for those who ate lunch, but it may have been that he couldn't afford both beer and lunch and so chose the one he preferred. His cane came tapping down the street, closer and closer, and Peabody leaped out in front of him and remarked rather loudly that it might be nice to have a glass of beer.

"Beer," said Thompson, shuffling past. "So who's keeping you from having one?" Up close this way you could tell he didn't wash as often as he ought, and you could see he was cross. They walked on toward Palmer's in single file, he in front and she following in silence, and at the corner they met Mrs. Morris coming toward them wrapped in her own isolation. Peabody caught at her coat and whispered loudly, "May I treat you to a glass of beer?"

"I hardly think so," Mrs. Morris replied, but the woman stood there and rambled on about how of course he was an unpleasant old man but she had to try to comfort him because after all a person had to do her best and there was some good in every human being . . . "Calm down," said Mrs. Morris. "Don't explain so much." They went into Palmer's, and she thought fleetingly of how often it seems to be the case that compassion derives from guilt and gives rise to contempt. Ready-made virtues struck her as being common, and she didn't like Miss Peabody. The tavern was empty. They sat at the bar, Thompson farthest in. He ordered three beers and a sandwich. The room was very dark, and long and narrow, with a door at one end. It was a thoroughly ordinary bar—shelves lined with bottles and those unnecessary, infantile objects that overload the shelves in every bar, a mirrored wall reflecting their own half-hidden faces, which became as incidental and anonymous as everything else in the room. The bartender served them in silence and turned his back.

"This is nice," Peabody whispered. "Believe it or not, Mrs. Morris, I've never been inside a real bar." The beer tasted bitter. She rested her arms on the bar, which felt nice for her back. People should always have high tables, it was restful and secure. The gaily colored shelves in front of the mirror gave her the feeling of being in a strange world far from St. Petersburg. Thompson ate his sandwich in silence. Without attracting attention, Peabody took out a five dollar bill and held it crumpled in one hand. It might be too soon and only make him mad. It wasn't long now until the Spring Ball, and had Mrs. Morris joined the Senior Club? She really ought to, there were so many ways to pass the time, hobby rooms and bridge and gymnastics and singing lessons. You had to be sixty years old was all.

"Really?" said Mrs. Morris.

"Yes. They do so much for senior citizens. Believe me, there isn't a place in the whole world where they do so much for us. Always summer and the whole ocean all around!" Mrs. Morris remarked that perhaps those details had a natural explanation, and Thompson said, "Another beer. And quick."

"Can you imagine, Mrs. Morris?" Peabody said. "I've never been in a real bar before!"

"Yes, you told me."

"Did I?" said Peabody uncertainly. "Maybe I did." She was quiet for a while and then mentioned that the Spring Ball was just as important as the Autumn Ball. Everyone danced at their own risk, and the spotlights rotated whenever they played a tango or a waltz. In the ballroom you were not allowed to drink or smoke. The gowns were fantastic. A lot of ladies took part in the great Cavalcade of Hats, which was a contest for the prettiest hat in St. Petersburg. "And Mrs. Rubinstein wins every time!"

"Potato chips," said Thompson. "And music. The first waltz is on Palmer's." The bartender started the jukebox, and the room was filled with leisurely, howling cowboy blues at full volume. Elizabeth Morris shuddered but said nothing. She had to get used to it, she had to. There was music everywhere and you couldn't escape it. Then a motorcycle blared around the corner and the good-looking boy from the *Bounty* dashed through the door and walked up to the bar. "Hi," he said. "Nothing for me?"

"No," said the bartender.

"No letter? Nothing? Nothing from Miami?"

"Not a thing," the bartender said.

Joe left again without looking at them, and his motorcycle roared on down the avenue.

"If you want to dance," said Peabody, "did I already tell you that if you want to dance the best thing is to sit on one of the benches right at the front? Then they know what you want."

"Who does?"

"The gentlemen."

"And where do the gentlemen sit?" Mrs. Morris asked.

"They circulate. There aren't so many of them . . ."

"They're all dead," Thompson explained. He had been listening the whole time. Peabody turned toward him suddenly and touched his arm, but Mrs. Morris said "Hush!" and she pulled back her hand. The jukebox scratched vacantly and let down a new record. It was rock. Maybe Thompson liked rock, he let his head sink in his hands. It was also possible that he was trying to protect his ears, or that he was simply tired. As unobtrusively as she could, Peabody pushed the five dollars under his elbow and he immediately lowered his arm to secure the money. "Three more," he said.

"Two," said Mrs. Morris. Did Miss Peabody like beer?

She guessed not much, not really, but she liked the drifting away. Would Mrs. Morris like to know what she bar. Her thoughts were light and untroubled, constantly did before? Before she came to St. Petersburg? But Mrs. Morris didn't answer. She just smiled vaguely from behind her sunglasses. Peabody turned toward the mirror behind the bar and thought, What difference does it make? She would never understand what it was like. Seamstress? she'd say. Really? In the lottery? What fun! I'll tell her we were a big family and now I'm the only one left. How sad, she'll say, and there we'll sit and we won't really have said anything at all. Her with her blue eyebrows and no eyes! Thompson began to groan again, and his head rolled slowly back and forth. Oh sure, thought Peabody angrily, just carry on any way you like. But I guess I don't have to be the only one who's nice.

"Good music!" said Thompson suddenly. "If it's gonna be noise then it ought to be noise, and they're keeping the beat for once, too. Peabody, put in some more money. I don't have any change."

Mrs. Morris made a sudden gesture but let it go at that. If they wanted noise, then let them have noise. Anyway, her headache had already started, down at the back of her neck. She clenched her teeth and waited for them to finish their beer.

When they got back to the Berkeley Arms, Thompson held the door for them. "Ladies . . . " he said, with chivalrous contempt.

Peabody. So her name was Peabody. A timid, self-centered little mouse of a person with no chin and tufts of white hair on her head. But of course she could have been even worse.

That evening, in a break between tourist buses, Joe drove to Palmer's again to check for mail. He explained that maybe it wouldn't even be a letter, just a card with a cross and an address. If there was a piece of paper with his name and a cross, then he would know what he had to do.

"We got lots of crosses," the bartender said, spreading paid checks across the bar. Every one of them was marked with a large cross. "What is it you're waiting for?" Joe replied that he was waiting for a signal to be off, to Miami or someplace else. It was very important. The driver from Las Olas said in his opinion it was probably a smuggling racket and some people ought to go visit their grandmother in Tampa for a change.

"You make me sick," Joe said. And the bartender said, "Jesus, nobody's normal any more, not the old geezers and not the newborn kids." And then the boy lay across the bar and screamed, "Hey you! You don't know a thing about Jesus!" and stormed out the door and roared off down the street with a screech of rubber. One of the customers sniggered. "Don't you get it?" he said. "He's one of those Jesus freaks who run around and let the taxpayers take care of them. They've got some sort of camp in Miami. They're all crazy about Jesus, it's some sort of a Yankee disease."

"Hippies?" the bartender said.

"No, not hippies any more. This is something else."

"Trouble," the bartender said. "The same trouble by a different name."

2

Linda had two hours to herself in the middle of the day, and she usually spent them in her room. It was a small, attractive room, entirely whitewashed and protected from the heat by the dense greenery in the back yard. Joe had fixed the altar above the bed and propped up the shelf so it would sit straight. He had run an electric cord to the lamp above God's Mother, who stood in the altar with her plastic flowers and the sugar skulls from Guadalajara. Joe respected the Madonna, although he was more interested in Jesus. They seldom talked about either one, and why *should* people talk about obvious things like the sun and the moon? The Madonna smiled constantly. Below her was Miss Frey's bell and the keys to the house. Linda took off all her clothes and lay down naked on the bed in perfect peace, with one hand under her chin. It was a good bed with durable coil springs. Pretty pictures began to float by, each one prettier than the one before. Mama first, and then Joe. Mama was big and calm and worked hard, and she didn't have to worry about her daughter, who was doing fine. She trudged through Guadalajara in her black dress with her basket on her head, into the shade of the market and back out into the sun again, taking care of her family. Joe was well off, with a steady job and a good salary. When Linda had thought about both of them, she let Silver Springs float by. She had never seen Silver Springs. There was a jungle river with water clear as crystal and monkeys frolicking on the banks. For a dollar you could ride on a river boat with a glass bottom and look at the fish swimming steadily by across the white sand. The jungle arched over the river from both sides, a soft green roof that continued far into America for hundreds of protected miles. Everything was protected by the government and there were neither snakes nor scorpions. Dear Madonna, Linda whispered, let me make love to Joe on the banks of the jungle river. And then by your grace we will wade out into the water and swim slowly away together, farther and farther away. She reached up and switched on the Madonna's lamp, not for the light but to pay respect. Then she folded her hands on her lovely stomach and fell asleep.

Bounty Joe came to her. He stood in the window open to the yard and called into her room. "Hi! They've forgotten me. They didn't mean it."

Linda lay still and looked at him. She said he had to be patient. It took a long time to find a house that didn't cost anything, and they wouldn't let people live in all the houses that were going to be torn down. The police in Miami were bad. He came in and sat down on the bed, facing the other way. "I can't wait any more, and I don't know where they are. They could be anyplace, but they'll never come here, no one ever comes here. Maybe they've found some place, a camp, a cave, a shack, how do I know? They found it a long time ago and forgot to write. And you know," he continued sternly, "you know as soon as I hear from them I'm leaving. There isn't much time. I'm leaving whether you come along or not!"

"I know," Linda said.

"And you're staying here."

"I have a good job," she said. "And they have given me papers right up to Christmas."

"Christmas!" Joe said. "That's ridiculous. He's going to come any day and you talk about Christmas and papers! It makes me mad to hear you talk like that when everything's about to happen. You've got the chance to be part of it, and you just let it go without blinking an eye. You could be there to welcome Him!"

"And if He does come," Linda said, "If He does come back, how do you know He won't come here instead? It could be St. Petersburg as well as Miami, the world is so big."

Joe stood up and started pacing back and forth in the room. He explained that the important thing was to be together, to be a group, and to have something certain to believe in. "There's no time to lose," he said. "He might come back in a week. They've figured out it's going to happen any time, so right now is the time to know what it's all about and to wait together. They play music the whole time. They play and talk to each other and dance while they wait. You can't wait all alone."

"Yes," Linda said, "I can see it's important. But you must watch out for the police in Miami. They come in black cars and drive along the beach and pick up everyone who has no place to live."

"You don't understand," he said. "There are thousands of them waiting on the beaches. They're like a family. They share everything." He tore open his jacket and showed her his Jesus sign on the inside, in red and purple and orange. JESUS LOVES YOU.

"Good," she said. "But you should have it on the outside of your jacket."

"I will! I'll have it all over! On my shirt and my trunks and all over if only they write to me! Didn't you see the cross on my bike? Don't you understand what's happening?"

It was hard to understand why Jesus made Joe so crazy. Maybe Jesus really was going to come back. And of course in that case he would have to be welcomed properly. He was temperamental and spoiled and never let you know ahead of time. The Madonna made no uncertain promises. She was simply there, always, eternally. An endless stream of miracles flowed from her bosom. "Dear Joe," Linda said, "don't be mad at me. I hope so much that He will come. You must be patient. They will write when they find out where He will land."

He looked at her face, which was always serene, and

all at once her submissive certainty seemed awful. "Why do you smile all the time?" he said.

"Because I am looking at you," she said. "Do you think we'll have time to visit Silver Springs before He comes?"

Thompson had a great weakness for Linda. She never told about the box under his bed, the cardboard box where he hid books, cognac, garlic sausage, and a can for cigarette butts. It was against the rules to smoke in the rooms. Thompson's room was impregnated with the stink of tobacco, mingled with garlic and, to some extent, unwashed clothes. Linda said nothing. She seemed to consider it natural that the rug was rolled up against the wall. She understood that the room gradually had to take on a character suited to the way he lived. She cleaned it very gently and with great consideration and never invaded his private life. This space, this extremely homey and evil-smelling space that represented Thompson's last barricade against the world, was the cheapest room at the Berkeley Arms, a narrow rectangle partially hidden beneath the stairs and furnished with odds and ends. He had hung his bedspread across the middle of the rectangle from one wall to the other and lived primarily in the window end. When he came in and closed the door behind him, the room was in darkness. The darkness divided the life that was forced upon him from the life that was conscious and private. In complete calm he waited to pass through the darkness toward forgetfulness and pleasure. Pictures and faces vanished and the voices were finally silenced. He stood still and waited. Eventually he could see the daylight outlining the bedspread, very faintly, and then he stepped forward and lifted the darkness to one side and entered his own essential space of bed, lamp, and chair. No one knew that Mr. Thompson could be happy, a fact that he took great pains to conceal. Women frightened him, these women who were everywhere and who died much too old. Over the years there was little they hadn't said to him, the way women do. They had shaped his silence. Today as he entered his innermost room, he put Peabody's money in the jar for private use. He sat down in the chair facing the window and looked into the same translucent greenery that shaded Linda's sleep. Both of them lived in a primeval forest, screened off from the world. He rolled the first cigarette of the day. The tobacco was coarse and unwieldy and a great deal slid off the paper. He pushed it into a little pile with his shoe to attend to later on, licked the cigarette shut, and lit it. Smoking gave Mr. Thompson a solitary satisfaction, the vindictive pleasure of things that are never shared. None of those veranda ladies, those old wives, those maidens and crones, those indescribable females, knew that he smoked. He deprived them of his secret joy, he punished them by smoking only in solitude.

Because Mr. Thompson was a woman hater, he thought about women a lot. His friend from San Francisco, Jeremiah Spennert, had never talked about women voluntarily, but if someone mentioned them he shook his head and smiled sadly, probably to indicate that they didn't know what they were doing and so

couldn't be held responsible. The subject Thompson
had chosen for today's meditation was: epithets worthy
of woman. For Jeremiah Spennert's sake, he wanted to
establish a designation that would express both dignity
and charm. He quietly bypassed those titles of honor
that by dint of taboo or overloaded symbolism cannot
be used in a factual assessment, such as mother, queen,
madonna, or even helpmate, which was a euphemistic
circumlocution for wife in literary or generally false
contexts. He dismissed those poetic arabesques that led
the mind astray and had no counterparts in the real
world, such as nymph, muse, dryad, etc., hesitated for a
moment at the beautiful word mistress, and then sent
her the same way. Working from the bottom up he
peeled off everything that smacked of shabbiness or har-
lotry, and somewhere in the middle he came across sisters, aunts, mothers-in-law and the like, but eliminated
them as being almost comic in an analysis of the present
kind. More and more names with feminine significance
forced themselves upon him. There were too many, way
too many. Thompson decided hastily that only one
"lady" and one "virgin" could be retained as the possible
bearers of sweet dignity—at least for the moment, as a
working hypothesis. He opened the window to get some
air and think. After a while he discarded both the lady
and the virgin. The only true woman was Linda. Linda
had not been corrupted by her sex. She had miraculously
and inexplicably escaped.

A faint smell of flowers drifted into Thompson's
room. The sun had moved toward the veranda but still
lingered in the foliage above the back yard. It shone

through the leaves and made pretty patterns of light and shade, motionless in the growing heat. The morning had been interesting. Every time he talked about death, at least one of the women would behave irrationally. Thompson recalled with pleasure the two ladies who had taken a beer with him at Palmer's, the large quiet one and the little uncertain one, the one with no chin, Peabody. He wished Rubinstein had been there. He had fixed her name in his mind, deeply and inexorably. It would have done Rubinstein good to sit in his silence, frozen out, whispering about trivial things, her with her disdainful voice that was impossible to understand—a satisfied voice, a stupid woman's self-satisfied voice.

It was quiet in the back yard. Johanson's garage stuck out between the bushes and the tool shed, but Johanson himself was nowhere to be seen. He's afraid of me, Thompson thought. Grandpa Johanson is very scared of me! The second cigarette of the day was finished, and he hid the butt in the can under the bed. It was execution time. The book was called *New Galaxies*. There was a typical Martian landscape on the dust jacket under the lending library's plastic cover. Thompson opened to where he had stopped and continued his microscopic notations in the margin. He used a fine ballpoint pen, and his handwriting was so excessively tiny that it looked as if an insect had dipped its legs in ink and scurried hastily across the paper. "Wrong!" Thompson wrote. "On page 60 there is mention of a lack of oxygen. Now we have a love scene (which is idiotic anyway) where the people have no trouble breathing. 'Quivering heat' is used three times on the

last four pages." He read on and underlined "the darkening heavens." "This author," Thompson noted in the
margin, "has a morbid fascination with 'darkening,'
'shimmering' (to some extent 'glowing'), and 'dusk.'
All of his male characters sneer, have steady eyes, and
express themselves either 'with amusement,' 'drily,' or
'with suppressed rage.' His women primarily pant and
whisper, when they're not screaming."

Mr. Thompson's commentaries had found their
most fertile soil in science fiction. When he was
younger, about fifty, he had assaulted poetry but found
that form of expression indefensible and not really in
need of commentary. After eight pages of *New Galaxies*,
Thompson set aside his morning game and took out a
book given him by his friend Jeremiah Spennert. Sometimes when his spirits were low he would read a little in
this voluminous work by G. W. F. Hegel, merely in
tribute and in memory of his friend from San Francisco.

3   It lasted for days. By Sunday afternoon Miss Frey still hadn't for-
gotten her defeat on the veranda—the childish, tasteless
scene, Mrs. Rubinstein's eyes and contemptuous tone
of voice, and her own escape into the vestibule and the
glass cage. A glass cage for the bookkeeping, ignored by
everyone. But she went on with her work, carefully
adding in the latest figures and checking them and
clipping together the receipts until everything was in
order. Now with the accounts for the week in a folder,
she went to Miss Ruthermer-Berkeley's room. She kept
one eye on Thompson's door under the stairs, right
where the corridor turned. He liked to stand in there
and wait, the old bastard, just inside the door. He knew
her walk and would jump out like a jack-in-the-box and
yell something, it didn't matter what, just to scare her,
and every time it scared her just as badly. I live in a

kindergarten, Miss Frey thought. No one realizes how much cruelty there is in a kindergarten. Thompson's door came closer. She passed it carefully, staring hard at the crack where it would open and running quickly through all the things you can say to an evil old man, haughtily, crushingly, impassively—but the door stayed closed and nothing happened. Miss Frey walked on to the corner room, where in a sudden spell of overwhelming weakness she rested her forehead against the wall and paused for a moment. Then she knocked on the door, and a high thin voice answered from within— Miss Ruthermer-Berkeley's sweet, ancient soprano.

The light in the corner room was always subdued. Daylight sank into the room through thick white lace and made no shadows. Around the oval table under the crystal chandelier stood five straight-backed velvet chairs. Miss Frey walked quickly to the table. She explained that here were the week's accounts as far as she had taken them, and she felt sure they were correct, even if all the receipts weren't in exact chronological order.

"Yes, my dear," replied the owner of the Berkeley Arms. "I understand. You've brought the accounts again. It's very nice of you." Every week the old woman went through the accounts. It was almost a courtly formality. Figures made her tired. They told her nothing any more, and Miss Frey knew it. The folder was opened in silence. Her small, dry hands, as thin as leaves, lifted the papers one by one, turned them slowly from one side to the other and let them sink to the table again. She's only pretending, thought Miss Frey, but she has to go through them anyway, she must. Her hands shook slowly the whole time. Ninety-three. How could anyone shrink to such a size? Dead birds shrank and withered the same way. Everything grew frail and dry and curled up its edges. It seemed to Miss Frey that the corner room had aged to the same state of parched fragility—the old chairs and tables on their slender legs, all the starched lace and worn silk, all the faded colors and the yellowed whites.

"Quite correct," said Miss Ruthermer-Berkeley. "Miss Frey, may I offer you a small glass of sherry?" But Miss Frey did not want any sherry. Was there something else on her mind?

"He still hasn't paid his rent. And Mrs. Rubinstein smokes in the TV room."

Miss Ruthermer-Berkeley sighed. "Let's relax for a moment," she said. "Perhaps we need a cup of tea. Yes, that's the proper drink for calm deliberation. Linda can bring us some tea."

They sat together quietly and waited for the tea. When Linda had served them, she stopped in the door and enclosed them both in her long radiant smile and then closed the door very quietly behind her. Miss Ruthermer-Berkeley confided that in the beginning she had been utterly confounded by Linda's smile. It had seemed to her that this overwhelming smile must be the prelude to some important confidence, that it was meant to introduce an announcement of an astonishing and pleasing nature. Now, however, she had come to realize that the smile was simply a phenomenon to view and enjoy, rather like some strikingly beautiful landscape. This insight in no way destroyed the sense of anticipation. "And over the years, Miss Frey, anticipation becomes a rarity that must be preserved with care."

"Yes," said Miss Frey. "Yes of course." Her labors for the Berkeley Arms were meaningless if no one saw and understood and cared, if no one ever criticized or praised or asked. It had been the same way at the bank —a faceless teller who never made a mistake, never ever a single mistake.

"Have a cookie," said Miss Ruthermer-Berkeley. "Yes, I see her as a lovely, peaceful landscape."

"Yes, yes," said Miss Frey. "She is pretty. She goes with the guard on the *Bounty*. His name is Joe. I've seen him leaving the Berkeley Arms very early in the morning several times."

"*Bounty*," the old woman repeated thoughtfully. "The guard on the *Bounty*. Do they need a guard these days?"

"For the tourists!" Miss Frey burst out in irritation. "The *Bounty*. The historical Mutiny on the *Bounty*, and now it's a movie ship, and they need a handsome man on board. Someone wrote a book about it. And the guard's name is Joe!"

"The book was written by Mr. Nordhoff and Mr. Hall," announced Miss Ruthermer-Berkeley carefully. "Do make a note that it was two gentlemen who wrote *The Mutiny on the Bounty*. You're tired, Miss Frey, and I'm afraid you take your responsibilities too seriously. Wouldn't you like to have a short vacation?"

Catherine Frey began to cry. She cried with her hands over her face and her elbows on the table, and all at once, as suddenly as she had begun, she stopped.

"Is it Mr. Thompson who is the most difficult?" the old woman asked.

"I don't know," she answered. "It's everything."

Miss Ruthermer-Berkeley stood up carefully and using her furniture for support she made her way to the bureau in the corner. "What you need now," she said, "is a little pill. I was given this box when I was young, by a beau who was studying medicine. As far as I can remember I've only used one pill, on some occasion. Most of the others I've given away when someone needed them, but we have four left. I will give them to you, Miss Frey. And I suggest that you devote the afternoon to your own comfort."

When Miss Frey had gone, Miss Ruthermer-Berkeley opened her French textbook. She had a long undisturbed afternoon and evening ahead of her. "Qu'est-ce que vous voulez?" she murmured caressingly. "Jamais. Jamais de ma vie. Toujours." How pretty it was. How pretty France must be.

It was not until after her ninetieth year that Miss Ruthermer-Berkeley began to ask herself whether her long life had not been lacking in what was once called a heart's desire. A much too rigorous upbringing may have had something to do with it, but essentially, she realized, it was all her own fault. Without sense or consideration she had striven for perfection and thus had lived with constant anxiety, anxiety for everything left incomplete the day before—work, duties, conversations —and anxiety for the day to come, which had to be shaped to suit her wishes and the demands she made on herself. Lost in the future and the past, she had not been able to live in her own moment. It was really a great shame, an omission that had probably made no one happy. But now they were all dead, and there was hardly time to mourn mistakes that were as old and as silly as that. Miss Ruthermer-Berkeley began to look for her disavowed desire and was pleased to discover that it was still fresh and unused, even if her possibilities for activity were now limited. She thoroughly enjoyed her study of the French language. Furthermore, the concept of a heart's desire can find expression in small things and sometimes in a single act—abandoning an old habit, for example, or permitting oneself the luxury of cutting off a futile or unpleasant line of thought. In the course of her ninety-second year, Miss Ruthermer-Berkeley developed a subtle capacity to channel memories and observations. By means of an involved system of locks and floodgates under the partial control of her subconscious, she let through whatever she thought agreeable and useful and shut off forever a large, feverish reservoir. She practiced entertaining new and irrational ideas. And at the same time, of course, the owner of the Berkeley Arms accepted a great many of those things that seem to secure their validity by virtue of their permanence, in other words, that accumulation of traditional conclusions that her ancestors carried with them because they could never find anything better.

Be that as it may, she was glad that all the bustle and anxiety had ceased.

The coolest place in the house was the vestibule, at the far end of which Miss Frey had her glass cage. The vestibule was almost always deserted, visited only by the Pihalga sisters who often sat beside each other behind a pillar. The long room was full of square white pillars and had been built to walk through on one's way to the second floor, or to the TV room or the veranda. Everything in it was white—the wicker furniture, Mrs. Higgins's Easter lilies, even the picture frames adorning inscrutable group photographs of staring white faces in standing, sitting, and reclining rows: old people in funny hats crowded together to be memorialized. To the right and the left of these tightly assembled groups the photographer had left quite an ample area of gray, indefinite background.

"This is a calm and attractive room," said one Miss Pihalga. Her sister did not stop reading, merely nodded. For an instant, their hands touched. Miss Frey didn't like them. Every time she looked up from her papers she could see them sitting there, dreadfully gaunt, their hawklike profiles bent over their books. No one knew what they read. No one knew anything about them except that they had come from a country in Europe on the Baltic Sea sometime in the twenties. They always moved into the vestibule when it got too hot on the veranda. Old crows, thought Miss Frey. Bad luck birds with long gray faces. God what a graveyard.

Since the Pihalga sisters had identical memories, identical opinions, and identical afflictions, they seldom spoke to one another. What they did say had almost the quality of a kind of quiet recognition, as acknowledgment of proximity and mutual justification. They read constantly. Sometimes when one of them found a turn of phrase, an interesting formulation, she would gently touch her sister's hand and the sister would lower her own book to read the indicated lines. And then they would read on in their separate books, their chairs very close together. This gentle, leisurely old age was perhaps the reward they felt they deserved after a life of unceasing change, constant upheaval, continual new people pushing into their lives though never getting close to them. It was not clear whether the guests at the Berkeley Arms respected the Pihalga sisters' final and unyielding way of life, or whether they quite simply found them boring. Nevertheless, they left them in peace, and never even discussed them. And maybe, too, there was a little fear, an aversion that couldn't be put into words. The sisters were terribly and patently old, not so much in years as in their apparent unconcern at the passage of time and at the fact that it might stop. Their appearance and their silence were reminders. No one asked them what they read, and the lending library jackets were all the same. Politics, claimed Mrs. Rubinstein, but she probably said that just to draw attention to herself.

Miami, thought Miss Frey. To go away. No crows in the vestibule, no damned old man in number four, no veranda. Warm sand and the hotel orchestra, and I'll have a Brandy Alexander on the terrace . . . She was looking for the guarantee for the refrigerator, pulling out drawers one after another and searching sloppily, then slamming them again and starting over from the beginning, no, not Miami. Attractive young people dancing and playing ball on the beach. Not Miami, I

won't go anywhere. She jerked out the top drawer and
there was the guarantee. She called the company, which
didn't answer, and then she remembered it was Sunday.
This was a day for rest and reflection. Without locking
the glass cage she hurried out of the vestibule and across
the back yard to Johanson's. She walked right in without knocking. "It's the refrigerator!" she said. "It's not
working. Here's the guarantee, so you can call them on
Monday."

He was watching TV. "Put it on the table," he said,
and she put the guarantee on the table and thought
fiercely: Some day when I'm no longer responsible for
anything at all I will never ever go into anyone else's
house! And never go into their rooms or past their
rooms! They're terrible and untouchable when they've
hidden themselves in their holes with their things. She
stood behind him and waited. After a while she remarked on how nicely he'd cut the lawn.

"I cut it Friday," he said without turning his head.

Miss Frey went out. It was Thompson, of course.
Thompson had been annoying Johanson again, stirring
up trouble like an evil spirit. Oh she knew! A nice man
like Johanson didn't get nasty simply because it was
Sunday. The back yard lay in heat and silence within its
walls. She walked in among the bushes, right up to
Thompson's window. Brazenly, with nothing to disguise
her face, she stared at him as he sat there in his window,
all crooked from a stroke God knows when, with those
enormous eyebrows that made him look like an ape.
Catherine Frey went closer. Without the least excuse,
she stared straight at him, relentlessly, the way an ani-

mal stares at its enemy, and just then she was frightful. A faint breeze stirred the leaves and altered the shadows, and for a moment it seemed to Thompson that the woman outside had shown her teeth. Or maybe she was crying. He dragged his chair farther back in the room and tried to go on reading. A few minutes later he went angrily back to the window but the back yard was as usual, green and untouched. Tigresses and jackal bitches, said Thompson to himself. I live in a jungle.

As a matter of fact, Thompson was not too much trouble as long as he kept to his room, but he upset the harmony of the Berkeley Arms by refusing to get along with Johanson. He made Johanson irritable, and he did it on purpose, they all knew that. For long hours as Thompson sat in the green half-light by his window staring out into the bushes in the back yard, he would keep close track of everything Johanson did. Between the leaves he could see the lawn and part of Johanson's house, its roof slanting against the garden wall on the Las Olas side. It was hardly more than a shed. It contained two rooms, plus the garage and an open tool shed full of gardening equipment and cases of soft drinks. Johanson was Swedish, and had come to this country from Gothenburg. He was sixty years old and comparatively happy with what he had done and what he was now doing. Quietly, without looking at people's faces, he tended to what needed tending at the Berkeley Arms. He took care of all sorts of things at his own pace, sometimes after a short conference with Miss Frey. His two rooms were neat and impersonal. He ate regular, unimaginative meals in one of them and in the

other he slept and watched TV, and felt neither anger
nor surprise at anything he saw. Johanson's presence was
comforting and important for the Berkeley Arms, for it
seemed to demonstrate that life was a normal proceeding
and could be regulated and adjusted. They seldom spoke
to him, but it was nice to see him working around the
house, wandering unhurriedly from place to place, always headed for something that was out of order but
would soon be functioning again the way they had
a right to expect. Thompson's annoyance at Johanson
was incomprehensible, even to Thompson. He sat in his
window for months and followed the quiet movement
from workshop to tool shed, the peaceful lumbering
back and forth with spades and rakes and electric cords,
cans of putty and paint, plant food and rat poison, always some kind of an important container being carried
somewhere in an important way. And as time went by,
Thompson grew more and more irritated, without
knowing why. Later, he tried to provoke Johanson,
tried to make him mad or shock him, but nothing upset
Johanson, not even insulting remarks about Sweden.
And then, one luckless day, Thompson discovered his
weak point. Johanson couldn't stand to have anyone
borrow his things. And he had a lot of things. He loved
his tools, which he kept well oiled and neatly in their
places, the garden implements that he polished, the
mysterious containers, the hoses, the cords, the machines,
yes, he loved the machines most of all, and especially
the van in the garage, which he kept spotless and cared
for like a baby.

That was how it all started. Johanson learned to fear

Thompson and lost his calm. It worked something like
this: Thompson would come limping toward him and
glance up from under his eyebrows. "Have you by any
chance got a . . . " he would say and pause sadistically.
"Could you by any chance get me a small chisel, a sharp
one?" And Johanson would see visions of his chisel
being destroyed in a tin can, in a lock, being prized into
God only knew what dreadful object for what awful
purpose and his face would twist in pain and he would
walk away.

Gradually, Thompson became more subtle. He
would want to borrow a plane or a precision drill. He
grew more and more inventive. He was never allowed to
borrow anything, but he struck terror into Johanson's
world. Each new question evoked a clear picture of perfection's ruin, and these visions of destruction pursued
Johanson and poisoned his quiet rounds through the
Berkeley Arms. The old bastard, Johanson thought. If
the old bastard knew anything about drills he'd want to
borrow my Double Diamond or my Stanley—and the
very thought went through his teeth like an electric
shock. Thompson sat in his window craning his neck
to see through the greenery. There he goes, Grandpa
Johanson in his garden, putting things in order. Everything's got to be a certain way, and he's got some in-
genious special tool for anything that doesn't work, a
tool that can only be used for one blessed thing.
Grandpa Johanson with all his rakes and wrenches!

A short time ago, Thompson had brought matters to
a head, to everyone's annoyance. The house hibiscus was
in bloom, and early one morning Thompson went out

and picked all the flowers. He found some contact cement in the garage and got into the van, and there, on the instrument panel, the old bastard had glued an hibiscus to every knob and button he could reach, although the point of it all seemed utterly impossible to tell. Johanson complained to Miss Frey. He had never done that before. And Miss Frey went to Miss Ruthermer-Berkeley. "Miss Frey, my dear," she said, "we mustn't be hasty. This cannot be labeled mental disorder in the usual sense." She looked at her hands the way she often did in moments of difficult decision and explained that the borderline between normal irrationality and complete derangement was very difficult to ascertain. No one could predict the course of an old person's thoughts and ideas. It was perfectly possible that in Thompson's mind there was some clear connection between "hibiscus" and "instrument panel." By which she did not mean to suggest in any way that Thompson's intentions had not been wicked. "But mental disorder, Miss Frey, is a serious matter, an accusation we cannot have on our conscience."

"But how do we know?" cried Miss Frey. "How do we know where the one stops and the other starts? He might just burn down the house some fine day!" Miss Ruthermer-Berkeley closed the discussion by observing that no one could ever be absolutely sure of anything, and that was the end of it. Afterward she thought how right she was to be firm, by virtue of her years and her insight. She wanted to defend the irrational surplus acquired in the course of a long life. She considered it a natural product of experience, and thus perfectly explicable and no cause for alarm. There were many people whose job it was to explain. For her, all that mattered was this: Our guests live here and have a right to expect protection. Outside of St. Petersburg there are all sorts of evil madness running wild, and we can't help that. But I have built a house over the kind of madness that is innocent, and it will be allowed to persist in peace for as long as I live.

4 Mrs. Morris's room was above Miss Ruthermer-Berkeley's. In the brief twilight she would go to the window and watch the mutiny ship *Bounty* light its lights. The rigging was illuminated every evening—those deep blue evenings that were such a long way from Nebraska. The street was as empty in the evening as it had been during the day, a broad, straight esplanade lit by vapor lamps. Sometimes it looked like a stage set on which the curtain had just gone up. The backdrop was the ship anchored at the pier with double rows of yellow lanterns in its rigging. For the visitor to St. Petersburg, it seemed natural to start by going aboard the *Bounty*. Everyone at the Berkeley Arms had been long ago. Mrs. Morris still hesitated. Maybe the *Bounty* was prettier from a distance. She wanted to hold on to her own picture of what a large sleeping ship was like.

At twilight on Good Friday, Elizabeth Morris woke up and shivered and thought it was morning. When she recognized the evening, she became unreasonably depressed. There was no cause to be depressed, not any more, and she knew that. There was nothing wrong with sleeping in the middle of the day. But every time she did it she had the same anxious feeling about lost worktime, the same bad conscience that wouldn't go away. The house was quiet, but the TV was on downstairs, just barely audible. Mrs. Morris put her coat around her shoulders and walked over to the window. The ship was lit. Background music, she thought. Gorgeous shot of the ship against the evening sky at the beginning of the movie, or maybe at the end. With my own poignant music. As a matter of fact, I wrote very good music.

As she gazed at the garlands of lights, her image of the great sleeping ship suddenly disappeared. All her evenings resembled one another like beads on a string, and Mrs. Morris realized that those points of light might just as well have hung above a gas station. That was interesting. She stripped the ship of its dreamlike quality and pictured an amusement park by the beach. It was easy, all she had to do was change the music. She thought "Silent Night" and turned the lights into Christmas decorations. Finally the ship was completely gone, and the backdrop no longer mattered. Elizabeth Morris left the window. She took her cane and went down the stairs as quietly as she could.

They were all sitting in the TV room. The Easter

program had come as far as Gethsemane and no one turned to look as she passed the door and walked out onto the veranda. The distant organ music followed her for a while, tearful and ghastly, and then all she could hear were her own broad shoes walking down the sidewalk and the hard intermediate beats of her cane in waltz time. The wind was blowing from the bay and the palm trees rustled. Not a soul was out tonight. Where the city ended she walked across the beach promenade toward the water. The pier lay in darkness, surrounded by high billboard walls, gigantic panels standing on strong legs and anchored down with cables. She couldn't see the bay. Mrs. Morris craned her neck and tried to decipher the enormous pictures and letters: Coca-Cola, Silver Springs, Sarasota Circus Museum, Moonlight Cruise in Tampa Bay . . . Aloha! The Dream of Tahiti— The Mutiny Ship Bounty. The ship was hidden behind a palisade of smooth logs. The gate and ticket booth were farther down. Inside the palisade, huge dark trees were swaying in the wind, and there was a sighing clump of sugar cane and the ground was strewn with fallen flowers. High above swung the moored ship's topmost lanterns. A movie camera could have captured them, leaving out the pier and the city and the whole world in order to catch only those lanterns and the calm, steady movement of those mast tops against the evening sky. A symbol of the sea, ships, and adventure, background music, fade out.

Just opposite, on the other side of the pier, was a gas station and the Senior Club, a low, gray concrete building. The enormous parking lot was empty. Some torn newspapers slithered and swirled across the asphalt in the rising wind, stopped, and then rose again in the same tight circle. It was cold.

Can you allow yourself the camera's right to discriminate and discard, to carve out a piece of beauty and forget about everything else? Is it acceptable? Yes, of course, Elizabeth Morris thought. Of course it is. Only it's utterly impossible.

She was starting to get cold and walked back to the Berkeley Arms the way she had come.

Bounty Joe and Linda were coming home from their Saturday evening out. They walked so lightly and in such close harmony that their movements looked like a secret, restrained dance. Joe's silver belt hung heavily over his hips. The buckle was two outspread hands pointing down. The Jesus message was on the inside of his jacket, only for himself. When they went out to dance, he never took his motorcycle. She was afraid of it. Now she was talking about Silver Springs again. She was always talking about Silver Springs—the jungle river, boats with glass bottoms, making love on the shore and swimming afterward, the white sand, the clear water, the wonderful National Forest, all for one dollar, and when were they going to go?

"One of these days," Joe said. "Sure we'll go, one of these days."

"Will we have time before He comes?" she asked. But Joe didn't want to discuss Him with Linda any more. He didn't want her sensible comfort. It was better to keep his longing to himself. She reduced his sorrow without making it easy to bear, and he wanted it the way it was.

All the windows were dark. Nowhere do the nights sleep as long as they do in St. Petersburg.

Silver Springs! Joe's rivers didn't creep through National Forests, they hurled themselves into the sea! His baptismal font was an Atlantic, and the holiness of the water so great that even an ordinary swimming pool could be powerfully blessed. Over in Miami they waded out to be baptized. Some of them walked slowly and others threw themselves into the surf as into an embrace, and they knew that never again could they be alone. The Jesus people stood on the beach by the thousands playing thousands of guitars in free and perfect expectation. He could see them! They stood still, but the wind lifted their long hair and their fringed clothing like ragged banners flying in the breeze, a whole coastline flying flags for Jesus! They hugged each other in the water and ran laughing up onto the beach, finally to begin their lives.

He'll be going soon, Linda thought. He'll give up his wonderful job. Everyone has to decide for himself, and you mustn't hold back someone who wants to go. An embrace is by the grace of the Madonna, and not a thing that can be kept.

They parted in front of the veranda, as always. She walked up the steps and he continued on down the street. At the corner he put his hand on the fence and swung himself over in one easy motion, into her garden.

Late one afternoon when the western sky had turned

yellow, Elizabeth Morris went back to the *Bounty*. On her way down to the harbor she caught sight of Mrs. Higgins, who was headed in the same direction. Hannah Higgins was carrying a plastic bag and looking for squirrels in the palm trees. From behind she looked more oval than ever, a black oval, and her head with its tiny bun of hair seemed to be perfectly round. She looked like a child's drawing. The palm trees too had been drawn by a child—crooked, bottle-shaped trunks with a vague disarray at the top. She stepped in behind a palm tree and started digging in her bag. Mrs. Morris quickened her pace and tried to hurry by.

"So you're out for a walk, too," Mrs. Higgins said. "It's kind of hard for me to look up in the air—everything spins around. Are there any squirrels today?"

"Not that I can see," Said Mrs. Morris staring at the crown of the tree.

"That's funny. But when I don't have any nuts with me, they're everywhere. Do you like nuts?"

"No, not especially."

"They get caught in your teeth," agreed Hanna Higgins warmly. "And having false teeth doesn't make it any better." She walked slowly on down the street, talking all the time. "This is a funny city, isn't it? Old people all over the place. What a clever idea to get us all together in the same place where we can enjoy ourselves without being in the way! There's so much to see here, and everything's so close. Last Sunday I went to the City Park to listen to the children's orchestra they had for us. Do you like music?"

"Sometimes," said Elizabeth Morris.

"Yes, sometimes, only sometimes, that's so true. Music is important, but you can't listen all the time. And the prettiest of all is the trumpet."

"Is it?" asked Mrs. Morris in surprise. Hannah Higgins started to laugh, that fresh laugh that was so vastly much younger than she was herself, and then still in high spirits she explained that her grandson played the trumpet. If he had played the saxophone, then that would have been the world's finest instrument. Such was life! At Bayshore Drive she stopped and looked to the right and the left, but there wasn't a car in sight. "Now we can cross," she said. Mrs. Morris was waiting to hear more about the grandson, but Mrs. Higgins only observed that the sky was yellow today and asked if she had been on board. If this was her first visit, she ought to go alone. "I'll wait for you outside," Mrs. Higgins said. "There's a nice bench and a cage full of monkeys."

They paid their money at the ticket booth and entered the Dream of Tahiti, which was small but very romantic. Huts covered with palm leaves amidst dense, subtropical foliage, where a person could buy all the souvenirs that a misdirected craving for beauty could shape from shell and coral, lava, bamboo, or alabaster, and over the entire area lay the sweet, suffocating odor of oiled wood. There were rest rooms and refreshment facilities half-hidden among the bushes. A pretty girl in authentic costume was selling plastic pirate ships and mermaids.

"I'll sit down here," said Mrs. Higgins. "Take your time, because there's a lot to see." The monkeys in their cage had round white faces with black eyes and black noses—small, melancholy death's heads. Mrs. Morris walked on. She looked at the totem pole and the outrigger canoe, which had spiny deep-water seashells glued to its bottom, and stopped in front of See Yourself in the South Pacific, a Lifesize Mr. and Mrs. Tahiti. They were plywood cutouts. He was wearing a blue uniform and she had on a grass skirt, and neither one of them had a head. For fifty cents you could give them your own head and have a picture taken.

And now, only now, did Elizabeth Morris raise her eyes and look up at the *Bounty*. She knew nothing about ships, but she could see that the vessel was magnificent. Gold, dark blue, and black, the rigging lifted toward the sky in incomprehensible beauty, and the pier around her vanished as she walked toward the waiting ship. Joe stood by the gangplank with a wreath of orchids in his hair. "Hi! Aloha!" he said and smiled professionally. He gave her an hibiscus. The flower was well made but hard to the touch.

"Hi," said Mrs. Morris. "Isn't it Hawaii where they say 'Aloha'? Do they say the same thing in Tahiti?"

"I don't know," Joe said. "Does it matter?"

So this was Joe with the motorcycle, Joe who loved Linda. Mrs. Morris took off her sunglasses and told him he was quite right. A greeting had its own value and didn't need to be translated. Then she went on board. The tourist bus from Tallahassee hadn't come yet and she was alone on deck. It filled Elizabeth Morris with awe, the austere, soft, balanced sweep of this enormous

deck and the perfection of its symmetry. All around her
—finally—she saw pure order, a world of absolute significance. Nothing was fortuitous and nothing unnecessary.
Almost reverently, Mrs. Morris went below. The sun
was low in the sky and filled the stern with a dark,
golden glow. Nowhere, she realized did people care for
the place they lived as they did on a ship. Every detail
was carefully shaped, every surface polished and absolutely clean. Brass and wood glistened like honey and
brown syrup. The tall windows threw rectangles of light
right up to her feet. And when you die, Mrs. Morris
thought with sudden interest, when you leave your
room . . . It was possible, it might just be conceivable to
leave an empty, sparkling room that was freed of everything and as clean as a deck. No litter and disorder, no
sign of debris from an exhausted life, habit and forgetfulness, the rubbish of days, the shameful slops of living.
All at once she remembered a phrase, "the slow creaking
of the vessel's hull"—probably from one of the adventure books she had loved so much. She walked on into
the wonderfully perfect room and saw the captain leaning over a map with his hands on the table, motionless
and worried. He was made of wax. No, she whispered.
She turned around and hurried away in embarrassment,
off through the dusky ship where she found them all,
one after the other, petrified in attitudes of attention,
fear, or wrath, all these gentlemen who had been dead
for so long and were now being displayed indecently in
wax. Mrs. Morris was frightened. She hurried through
the hold and couldn't find the stairs. From the ceiling
the loudspeakers came alive with ukulele music that

melted and dripped on her with its inescapable niceness. She came to blue, fluorescent light and there lay a man in his bunk, in his private spotlight, a lonely, dying man. His eyes stared and his mouth had fallen open. One arm hung over the edge of the bed, a ghastly yellow arm with black hair. They had had him drop his bottle, and a dark fluid seemed to run across the floor. Mrs. Morris turned and found the stairs. Up on deck she walked over to the railing and rested her forehead in her hands.

"Aloha," said Bounty Joe. "Are you all right"

"Yes I'm all right," said Mrs. Morris. She tried to catch sight of Hannah Higgins and the bench by the monkey cage, but a lot of people came in from the pier and got in the way.

"The old lady didn't feel well," said Bounty Joe. "She went home. I got her a taxi."

"Was she very sick?"

"I don't know. She didn't want me to come along. I would been been glad to go with her, I do that all the time. This sort of thing happens a lot, believe me."

"I'm sure it does," said Mrs. Morris. "Aloha." On the way home she saw a lot of squirrels. Almost everyone was out on the veranda when she got there.

"Nothing to worry about," said Miss Frey. "She's feeling better and has everything she needs. But long walks are not a good idea. I've said you should go to the park, but not to the beach, it's too far."

Mrs. Morris went upstairs and knocked on the door. "It's only me," she said.

"Come in, come in," said Hannah Higgins. She lay

under a quilt and was white around the eyes. It was because of the palm trees. "I shouldn't look up. It's not good for me. I know it's not good for me. But I threw up a little and now I feel better. How did you like the wax museum?"

"It was very well done."

Mrs. Higgins made herself more comfortable and stared up at the ceiling. "Funny knots in the wood," she said. "I didn't like the wax figures either, but we liked the boat." Mrs. Morris walked slowly around the room. A great many photographs and curios, far too many souvenirs and lovely tropical scenes, and in the middle of the wall a large velvet painting of dolphins against a sunset. It was covered with glitter. It seemed unlikely that Mrs. Higgins had picked it all out herself. She had a grandchild who played the trumpet, maybe she had another grandchild who was a sailor.

"Fourteen grandchildren," said Mrs. Higgins from the bed. "Those are their pictures you're looking at, and their parents too. But it wouldn't help you much for me to tell you who was who. They've all turned out so well." She paused. "My grandson who went to sea is studying for his captain's papers."

Mrs. Morris went from picture to picture and finally she came to the foot of the bed and asked what sort of music the trumpet player played.

"Rock," said Hannah Higgins very tiredly. "Progressive rock." She closed her eyes. After a little while Elizabeth Morris went to her room where she put some new blue make-up on her eyebrows, bluer than usual.

5 Mrs. Rubinstein sat under the dryer at the hairdresser, her white hair piled in a complicated crown. She filled the whole chair, narrowing at the top like a walrus, and the line that described her breast and slightly rounded back was long and billowy. She was very stately. Her thoughts were large and dark, turning backward in time and circling, as always, around her family—her enormous and distant family. Mrs. Rubinstein was a strong woman, and she had dominated them to the second and third generation. Now they were on their own and seemed to be doing all right, since she so seldom heard from them. Or else they didn't tell her how bad things were. Whatever they did, she always saw them as a mass of aimless activity against a dark background, like those Biblical engravings full of light and shadow that depict the children of Israel streaming through the desert,

demonstrating around the golden calf, or reveling in the land of Canaan.

She thought about the long years during which her will and intellect had formed new Rubinsteins and even the people they married or were forced to live without. When she thus considered time and effect and the chains of reaction set off by her own radiant energy, plus the family tendency to move away to strange lands, always stranger and more distant, there to perpetuate her seed, it seemed to Mrs. Rubinstein that she bore the whole earth with her like a heavy weight. It was nice the way the passage of time brought all the details together into a single picture. Events, faces, words drifted closer and closer together into the great crawling mass of progeny that filled the earth. Only Abrascha was completely distinct. Abrascha's childhood, youth, and middle age, they never paled.

"It's too hot," Mrs. Rubinstein said, and the hairdresser turned the dryer down to half and handed her some magazines. The one on top had a bathing beauty on the cover. The girl was playing in the waves. She had long black hair, a lot of white teeth, and a little round belly that might grow large in time, maybe with a new Rubinstein, the old woman thought—they're everywhere. She lit a cigarette and peered through the smoke into the mirror, appreciatively, but with a certain sadness.

In the evening it began to rain, lightly but steadily and firmly. It was a real spring rain that might last all night. The air grew pure and sweet and the garden became

very fragrant. The lights were lit on the verandas all
along the avenue and everyone came out and sat in their
chairs to watch the rain fall. Thunder rumbled in the
distance and there were several flashes of lightning
above the *Bounty*. Evelyn Peabody sat with her hands in
her lap. The smell of wet grass and the sigh of the rain
carried her far back in time and she could remember
without pain. As always, she thought about her father.
She loved him. He took them on a picnic every Sunday
and he'd be eager and excited and talk all the time. He
loved the Excursion Concept but had no organizational
talent. There were too many of us, Peabody thought,
and we were too little, and Mama worried all the time—
there might be snakes and ticks and it might rain . . .
Papa would run around setting things up. One time
when it was cold and windy, he found us a barn. And
one time he tried to build us a hut out of pine boughs,
but it was too much for him. "My dear little family!
Here we are in the bosom of Mother Nature! Throw
yourselves down in the grass, in the shade of these great
trees!" He used to talk like that when we'd go on an
excursion. "Children, my dears, for years I've been
searching for a genuine forest spring. What a joy it
would be to show you a thing of such beauty. So far, to
my great sorrow, I have not found one. Can you forgive
me?" And then it started to rain, and he gathered us
under a huge tree and Mama said if there was lightning,
a big tree was the most dangerous place to be. And once
I tried to tell her that we liked danger, but I don't think
she heard what I said. Papa was often sad on the way
home. How is it possible that they're all dead?

The Pihalga sisters came out and started reading. Miss Frey brought out her drawer of beads and threaded a blue one, a white one, and two pink ones.

One time he bought an outboard motor, a very small one that almost never worked. We were going to take a trip down the river in the boat, but he couldn't start the motor. "We'll row," he said. "Anyway, rowing is a much more honest way to travel." Mama said it looked silly to row when you had a motor, and so he let go of the motor and it sank to the bottom of the river. All that money! "Yes," Papa said, laughing as hard as he could, "and there it is on the bottom of the river and now we can row to our heart's content!"

Quite unexpectedly, Miss Peabody was struck by a sharp pang of loss and clenched her hands and leaned forward in her chair.

"Aren't you feeling well?" Mrs. Morris asked.

"Oh no, there's nothing wrong with me," said Miss Peabody, turning her head away and sitting up straight again. This woman with the blue eyebrows who was afraid to show her eyes! This woman who was afraid of music!

Mrs. Morris said how nice the rain was, but the little mouse person said nothing and began to crochet. So she asked what she was crocheting, but got no answer. Now I've been too quiet again, thought Elizabeth Morris. She closed her eyes and listened to the rain. On the other side of her, Thompson let a horrendous fart.

"That's a good sign," Hannah Higgins remarked. "Linda says he's been constipated for a week and won't take anything for it. I think a change in the weather would be good for all of us." The thunder rolled closer, and Frey started talking about hurricanes, especially the one in sixty-nine that tore the tops off half the palm trees on Bayshore Drive. And when the flood tides went out they just stood there like miserable stumps, and it took so long for a palm tree to recover!

"It's true," Mrs. Higgins rocked. "And the poor hotel!"

"They had plenty of warning."

"Yes, they did warn them."

"And afterwards when the water dropped!" Mrs. Higgins stopped rocking and waited mournfully.

"And afterwards! Farther up on shore! They found old people caught in the trees!"

"Were they torn to pieces?" Thompson asked. "Had they come apart, or were they still in one piece? How could someone get caught in a palm tree?"

"They were dead," said Miss Frey very curtly.

"Rain!" Peabody burst out suddenly. "Rain. It's a bad sign. We could have a hurricane any day!" She was talking very fast. "Yes indeed, Mrs. Morris, you just don't know about Florida. It's a very dangerous place if you don't know what's what, I can tell you that. I've been in hurricanes, and I know what it's like! One time I ran the news to a place where they didn't have a radio and didn't know it was coming and saved thirty people's lives!"

"What are you talking about?" Frey cried. "That's not true. You never told me that. You can't run!"

"I rode my bike! And if you think I've told you everything that ever happened to me, why you're very much mistaken! That was a long time ago, back in fifty-four!"

"You were still in Tennessee in fifty-four, stitching hems," Frey said.

"Girls, girls," said Hannah Higgins, and Thompson repeated his questions. "What did they look like? Were they torn to pieces? How could anyone get caught in a palm tree? They must have been speared through the middle," he went on triumphantly. "I can just see it—a senior citizen skewered on a palm tree. It's surrealistic!"

"He's absolutely phenomenal," said Mrs. Rubinstein. Thompson put his hand behind his ear. "What did she say now?" he whined. "What'd she say?" And Miss Frey leaped to her feet and sent beads bouncing all over the veranda floor and yelled, "You're phenomenal! She said you're phenomenal about reminding us of death! You think it's funny when people are torn to pieces. You think tragic things are funny!" Mrs. Rubinstein remarked that she hadn't really meant to say all that. She only meant to compliment Mr. Thompson's barbaric and vivid imagination. Silently she considered the advisability of a small indelicacy in connection with the naked palm trees pointing toward the sky, but decided against it. Not right at the moment, perhaps.

"There's a white one," said Mrs. Higgins. "It rolled right up to the edge."

Peabody was helping Frey pick up the beads. "Don't pay any attention to him," she whispered. "You mustn't let a poor old man get on your nerves . . . You have to try to understand . . ."

"Nerves!" Frey hissed. "Understand! You're just everybody's little friend, aren't you?"

The rain continued, and one after another they all went into the house. Only the Pihalga sisters sat on, reading in the poor light.

Later that night, Thompson knocked on Linda's door. "Linda?" he yelled. "Do you have Joe in there?"

"Yes," she said.

"Then I won't come in," he said. "I just wanted to tell you I finally took that pill, and it worked wonders! Just now, a minute ago."

"How nice," Linda said. "That is good news, Mr. Thompson."

"Yes," he said. "I thought you'd be pleased. Say hello to Joe." And he went back to his room.

The next day was unusually pretty. Although the sun was well up, the night's moisture lingered in the greenery between the houses, and there was no wind to shake the raindrops from the trees. As soon as Frey unlocked the glass cage, Peabody hurried up with her rent in one hand. "Hi!" she called out. "Are you in a better mood today?" She showed her front teeth in a hasty little smile that always made Frey think of a color cartoon and laid out her money in the window. "Isn't it funny? I'm always first with the rent. I never forget! Who would have believed it?" And while Frey opened drawers and wrote out a receipt, Peabody began her rapid, almost breathless description of how it had been, of how it had happened and how it had felt the day she won the lottery and couldn't believe it was true and called the radio station over and over again to be sure and wept for joy. "Oh, Catherine, I didn't really believe it until I saw it in writing and had the money in my hands. But of course by then Papa had been dead for a long time, and all the others too." The eyes that cried so easily filled anew with tears, and Frey said, "Fine. I know. Here's your receipt."

"Are you angry with me?" Peabody said, and tried to peek in through the window.

"No, no. That was wonderful. Fantastic."

"Yes, fantastic," said Peabody thoughtfully. "Catherine? What did you mean by what you said yesterday? Did I say anything that you didn't . . . I mean, what was it I said? I've lain awake for hours. For hours!"

"I don't know," Frey said. "It was nothing."

"Are you sure?"

"It was nothing."

"Really? Don't be so sure." Peabody rested her arms on the window and thought about what they call blind chance. After a while she remarked that the best part of all had been the sense of justice. "The last shall be first, that's what it says, isn't it?" She was using her plaintive, childish tone of voice. When Frey didn't answer, she said it again. "Isn't that right? Isn't it? The last shall be first?"

"Evelyn, dear," Frey said, "maybe they will and maybe they won't, but right now I've got to finish these accounts." Peabody was quiet for a while. "Catherine?" she said finally. "You don't look well. You ought to get a check-up. You ought to have regular check-ups at your age. You ought to take better care of yourself. A lot of people have noticed that you don't seem well, and I often worry about you."

"You do? You worry about me? Do you lie awake at night and think, my poor friend Catherine, if only I could help her and protect her!" Peabody turned red in the face. "You shouldn't be sarcastic!" she said. "I protect you more often than you think! I'm always loyal. I always say you're okay. It's just nerves, I say. I defend you against all of them!" The narrow little mouse face was pressed against the glass, and after a while the childish voice went on. "It's just the truth. I just want you to know the truth. You've got the right to know!"

"What did they say?" whispered Catherine Frey. "What did they say? And who said it?"

"I don't have the right to tell you that! I can't tell on them after all. It just seemed to me you had a right to know the truth."

"Right!" cried Miss Frey and stood up. "Right! The truth! And who the hell gave you the right to tell it?" Peabody clapped her hands to her mouth and ran off into the vestibule, fled toward a pillar and then staggered on toward the stairs. She'd been frightened. Tears rushed to her eyes, and the beautiful day was spoiled before it began. On her bed, alone with her beloved photographs, she tried to understand and forgive. It was just too bad about Catherine Frey. Distrust was a poison that made a person shrink up and lose all contact with real life.

On Monday, Abrascha's letter came. He was meticulous. Every letter was mailed on one of the first three days of the month, depending on when he could get some time free from business. Each letter contained a drawing done by the most talented grandchild. Mrs. Rubinstein doubted the talent, at least in the artistic sense. She did not save these drawings, nor the letters. They were all much alike. Libanonna was taking piano lessons. The business had survived some crisis, and Abrascha was hoping for this or that, the weather was good or bad, they were looking forward to a visit, a conference, a holiday, or else they had had a visit, a conference, a holiday, hello from all of us, love, and always mailed one of the first three days of the month. Mrs. Rubinstein knew that her own letters were similar, disgustingly similar. One day when a baby hurricane kept all of

St. Petersburg indoors, Mrs. Rubinstein was seized by a sudden mood and began a letter to her son.

My dear Abrascha, she wrote. My dreadful son. We are very like one another, although you did not inherit my intelligence in the broad sense of the word. In any event, after a long, strenuous, and observant life with your mother, you ought to have figured out that I detest platitudes more than silence and half-hearted, impersonal comments more than brutal truths. Have you never stopped to consider that these piano lessons, these scheduled business conferences, these picnics and dinner parties with influential persons, as you describe them, are like grass in the wind to me, your mother, Rebecca Rubinstein? Give me proof that my grandchild is a genius and not just a curly-headed darling who torments your guests with uninteresting accomplishments. Tell me clearly, in dollars and cents, how the business is doing. Describe nakedly who you have cheated and who has cheated you, *khaloshes*. Send me no vague Sunday paintings without color! Influential persons indeed! Who? How did you meet them? What were you hoping for, and what came of it? Have you no imagination? And if you do, what do you waste it on? Why do you never mention the wife I chose for you? Is there anyone who can understand, appreciate, the way I do, your mother? It is unpleasant for you to hear, but no one on earth can perceive and feel the subtleties of what you live through, of what you achieve and neglect, the way I do. Is it hard for you to forgive? Were the alternatives I gave you too distinct? Can you not forgive me the harvest you reap on what I sowed? *Are* you a success? I know nothing. You send me lists of names, the names of insignificant relatives. The more distant they are from the fountainhead, the paler they become. Why do you tell me about how colorless they are becoming? Do not remind me of this embarrassment, of this steady loss of vitality. Silence is better. Find new words to express your concern for my health, and reduce your adjectives to a sum you can be the master of.

My beloved son, the capacity to miss another human being is a rare gift. We are not blessed with its pain. Abrascha, remember that I shaped your lives in perfect awareness of the fact that I alone knew your direction. Why may I not know which way you are growing? *Are* you growing?

Sholom! Never write because it is the day to write!

Your loving,

Rebecca Rubinstein

She read through the letter carefully, put a comma here and there, nodded approvingly, and tore it into tiny pieces.

7 Elizabeth Morris did not go back to the ship, but in the evenings she would look at the lights in the rigging through her window. She began to amuse herself with a new distraction, an absent-minded game—replacing conversation with the written word. Silently exchanging messages written down on pads of paper. Handing someone such a note would in itself be a token of respect—a Japanese bow to indicate that one was approaching another person's orbit with discretion. A voice opening up in the middle of a face can be frighteningly obtrusive—the unconsidered words of the moment, demanding an immediate reply. There has to be time to think, thought Mrs. Morris, an opportunity to reflect. The time that writing requires, a mute communication, would leave space for deliberation. Almost everything we say is marked by haste and thoughtlessness, habit, fear, and the need to impress one another. So much needless

triviality, exaggeration, and repetition, so many terrible misunderstandings. Mrs. Morris looked at the ship and went on with her game. Title: Conversation on a veranda. Disposition: Excitment, caution, style. Like a game of chess, but with more room for the unforeseen. She had nothing against strong emotions as long as they were justified by formulation and abstraction. And then the next day you could meet one another without embarrassment.

For that matter, what was to keep you from writing simply, "Look it's raining," or "I don't want to talk," or "To hell with everything."

The only worthy playmate Mrs. Morris could think of was Mrs. Rubinstein. But that sophisticated lady had her place at the opposite end of the veranda and was therefore out of reach. To move your rocking chair is an unforgivable insult in St. Petersburg. The new arrival had no idea how important the rocking chairs were. The chair you got was final. Gradually you learned the unspoken rules of the house and followed them strictly. Only death could move the rocking chairs in St. Petersburg.

Mrs. Morris imagined what it would be like to sit beside Hannah Higgins. It was a lovely idea, but of course it would make the new game utterly unnecessary. Why would anyone play word games with Hannah Higgins? She didn't think of Thompson and the grim pleasure they could have given one another.

Now, at the approach of Easter, Elizabeth Morris grew restless. She left the Berkeley Arms and took walks to strange, distant parts of the city. She had strong legs and used her cane mostly as an affectation, swinging it up and out in time with her pace. The cane was something of a challenge and never an appeal. She chose streets with a lot of traffic and times of day when people were rushing home from work. The people coming toward her swerved to either side—it was like walking through a rapids. Sometimes she would stick to just one street. The crosswalks were difficult. Dammed up for a red light, the cars would rest on their haunches and then leap forward before she had time to get across. She was afraid of them. She would cross the street with her eyes fixed on the light, and it would change too soon. Green jumped almost immediately to yellow, and every time she felt furious and hurt and made it up onto the sidewalk with her cane scratching at the pavement like an anxious hen with her tail feathers all askew. And the whole time, incessantly, all through this busy, unfamiliar city, Mrs. Morris was pursued by music. These working people played it constantly, pouring out music like waterfalls, carrying it with them. A transistor in a hand came blaring down the sidewalk and met another one going the other way, sometimes playing the same thing, sometimes chaos. Car radios gushed out music that vanished in a roar when the cars leaped forward through the green. From open windows, from jukeboxes, from loudspeakers in department stores, music and the spoken word spilled violently through the streets.

Sometimes her headache would start a little later than expected. But then it would hammer mercilessly deeper and deeper into the back of her head, and she would let it be and walk on through a storm of demented, uncontrolled music, a storm that she had to get through. Sometimes she got tired. There were no benches or parks in this part of town so she would sit on a step or a curb. No one paid any attention to her.

Mrs. Morris listened for a whole week. She waited with a patience that was offset by curiosity. Then she found the drills. They were at the edges of the city, the still uninhabited areas along the coast. She would take a taxi and get out at a landfill or a road under construction. In her bright walking dress with a scarf on her head, she would watch the drills and the excavators that crawled about slowly changing direction and yawning and lifting and heaving in a cloud of dust and the trucks that constantly came and went. The men working on the embankment got used to the sight of the old, observant woman. The embankment grew in huge, enclosed blocks, a new foundation for new buildings for St. Petersburg.

One day while Elizabeth Morris was sitting by the bayside listening to the drills, she realized that something important was finished. She stood up and walked over to one of the trucks. It had just dumped its load and was ready to drive away. On a page of her notebook she wrote: "My name is Morris and I'm tired. My address is the Berkeley Arms on Second Avenue. Would you please drive me home?" The driver leaned down out of his cab and read the note. "Sure thing, grannie, climb on in," he said and thought to himself, The poor old thing is deaf and dumb and now she's got herself lost. They drove in toward the city with the truck radio playing popular music. Mrs. Morris knew she wouldn't be going back to the streets or the drills. She sat there in a great calm, and the music didn't bother her. She felt ready for a private silence that sounds could no longer torment. Just then something happened that made her very happy. A trumpet solo, clear as a spring, poured from the driver's radio—*Petite Fleur*, with an almost unbearable purity, slow, and passionately innocent. Mrs. Morris picked up her notebook and wrote eagerly, "Sidney Becket, trumpet!"

The driver read it. "Does he live at the Berkeley Arms?" he said. "Is he a friend of yours?"

"The music," Mrs. Morris wrote. "Listen!" But a commercial stopped the music. They drove up Second Avenue, and the truck driver said that friendship was a fine thing, indeed it was. The truck stopped at the Berkeley Arms and she touched his arm and smiled.

"Here you are safe and sound," the truck driver said. "You'll be just fine. A little nap on the veranda and you'll be right as rain."

8 One day shortly before the Spring Ball, about four o'clock in the afternoon, one of the Pihalga sisters became violently ill and was taken away in a silent ambulance. That evening, her sister came back from the hospital, climbed the steps to the veranda, and stopped at the top. They all sat there waiting in the cool evening air.

"I have a message from my sister," she said. "My sister said to tell you all hello. Now we have to return all our books to the library. The books have to be returned. We have always been very careful with the books we borrowed." Miss Pihalga looked around as if she were glancing out across an ocean and then she went into the house.

Peabody started wailing about the poor lonely sisters, but no one paid any attention.

The one Pihalga sister came back out carrying a

shopping bag full of books and walked up the street toward the library.

"They close at eight thirty," whispered Miss Frey.

The silence of the city was complete this evening, the silence of a sanctuary. Very, very distantly, no more than a vibration, came the echo of the traffic on the highways. Some of the rocking chairs were rocking slowly, but no one spoke. After half an hour Miss Frey went in to her glass cage to call the lending library. She came back out onto the veranda and stood by the balustrade and grasped the rail tightly with both hands. She informed them that Miss Pihalga had returned the books to the library and then died, the same way her sister had done.

"What were they reading?" Thompson asked. Miss Frey declared that it was a loss for all of them. The old sisters had lived at the Berkeley Arms so long. "We've all lived together so closely," she said.

"Oh we haven't either," Thompson said.

"And now it's my duty to inform Miss Ruthermer-Berkeley, as gently as I can. As you know, she's very old." Miss Frey went into the vestibule. A flood of life rose within her and colored her cheeks. Her whole body was trembling.

The owner of the Berkeley Arms took the double death calmly. She observed that the sisters had chosen to depart this life very discreetly, and that the almost mysterious simultaneity of the event gave it a certain style of its own. "I believe," said Miss Ruthermer-Berkeley, "I begin to believe that a person really can die from such a thing as grief. Our predicament, Miss Frey, is that that means of making an exit is no longer open to us. Grief, Miss Frey, is very pure and strong, and it requires a great love. It is not the same as being unhappy."

Frey thought the old woman talked too much. "Well," she said, "anyway they're dead, and there's nothing we can do."

"No, there's nothing we can do. Nothing that's done can ever be undone or be forgiven."

Miss Frey asked if that was meant to be a reproach, and Miss Ruthermer-Berkeley said, "No, not a reproach, a reminder. None of us liked them and none of us wanted to know about their lives. We are being admonished to be more careful with each other. It is much too easy to poison one's memories."

Miss Frey went back to the veranda and Thompson immediately said, "What were they reading? What happened to the books? Did she have time to turn them in?" Miss Frey replied that no morbid details could alter what had happened.

"Listen, whatever your name is," Thompson said, "I don't want to know if their hearts wore out or their brains stopped working or what happened to their poor stomachs, I just want to know what books they took back to the library because I think it's important."

Across the street at Friendship's Rest they had turned on their record player—an operetta from the nineteen thirties, as usual. Frey walked down the steps and across the street. The music stopped.

"And what do we do now?" Peabody whispered.

"Are they going to take away their rocking chairs? Should we all change places, or should we just sit farther apart? And is it all right to go to the Spring Ball so soon afterwards?" Hannah Higgins replied that there were always the same number of rocking chairs no matter what happened, which was a great comfort. Anyway, Evelyn shouldn't worry about it now, since the Scriptures said that sufficient unto the day was the evil thereof.

That night when Joe came into Linda's room, the lamp by the shrine was lit and he noticed that she had painted the Madonna black—all her clothes and even the scarf on her head. She said it was bicycle enamel and that Johanson had given it to her.

"But why?" Joe said. "What's she supposed to be black for? That's crazy. I've never seen anything like that. Is it because those old ladies died?"

"No," Linda said. "Funerals are white. They're always white." She had painted her black because she felt like it. She just decided to, all by herself. She took her clothes off and folded each piece of clothing on the chair but hung her dress carefully over the foot of the bed.

"You always wear black," Joe said, and although he didn't want to, he started thinking about Linda's mother again. Mama who was always near, Mama who dressed in black. It was a color they were crazy about down in Mexico. Mama's mouth must be a thin line, a tight-lipped mouth, the way it gets when you swallow too much and get your own way by secret means. A tremendous martyr, Linda's mother.

"Aren't you going to get undressed?" Linda said.

Black, they were crazy about black. She could have come to him in pretty colors. There were so many—red and yellow and pink and bright green and all the other exciting colors that make birds love each other. But as time went by he got used to it, and eventually black became the color of desire. He desired Linda in black.

"I'm the one who fixed the light for you," he said.

"Aren't you coming to bed?" Linda asked.

"And who's it burning for, the light I fixed? Is it for the Madonna, or for us, or for your Mama?"

"Everyone," Linda said. "You must wait for a while and then everything will be fine." She looked past him when she smiled, far past him, and her eyes were like the eyes of an angel or a concubine. Bounty Joe threw himself down beside her and whispered, almost frenziedly, "Jesus loves you!"

"Yes of course," Linda said and nodded gravely. "I'm sure He does."

There was a Madonna in black. Linda knew her well. The black Mother of God answered prayers much better than any other Madonna, and her house was always full of people praying. She was most compassionate toward those who were still young, and she knew that their childish wishes were not always for the best. And therefore, in her wisdom and her foresight, she listened and gave answers that people didn't always understand at first but which were never wrong. And now she had taken charge of the letter that was to come to Joe.

At midnight, Miss Peabody came to Room Six and asked

if she could borrow some sleeping pills. She was out. Mrs. Morris said she didn't have any. If she couldn't sleep, she usually read or sat by the window.

"I can't stop thinking about them," Peabody said. "Honestly, I feel so bad. We never cared about them the least little bit. Think about it. We don't know anything about them at all, except that they came from Europe somewhere, from some Baltic country. And what does that tell us? Nothing. We didn't even know their first names."

"No," said Mrs. Morris. "And now we feel bad about it. It'll pass, Miss Peabody, we'll get over it."

"I don't know," Peabody whispered. "I don't know that I'll ever get over it." She was wearing a nightgown covered with frills and lace, somewhat faded and shapeless, a very Peabodyish nightgown. Elizabeth Morris pulled up the covers and looked at the clock.

"Death and suffering," said her guest and sat down on the sofa. "We never have any peace. If it's not one thing it's another. Mrs. Morris, I'm so tired. Things go wrong for everyone, and afterwards I always think maybe I could have done something to help."

Mrs. Morris observed that probably she could, but that it was easier to comfort oneself with the Pihalga sisters' obvious desire to be left in peace. "And we run first to the person who makes the most noise and forget about the ones who live in silence."

Peabody stared at her. "I don't feel well," she said. "I'm afraid. You never know when it will happen, it could come anytime!"

"Yes of course," said Mrs. Morris angrily. "We could

die at any moment, and it doesn't make that much difference." Her guest began to snivel.

"Please, Miss Peabody, I beg you, don't. When I say it doesn't matter very much, why, that's the truth. It simply ends, and old as we are, it probably won't take that long."

"It won't?" whispered Peabody. "How long? Tell me more. Don't be mad . . ."

"This is a silly and pointless conversation," said Elizabeth Morris. "And it's late. As far as I can see there's only one thing to worry about, and that's not to scare people when you die, and not to give them a bad conscience. Considering what a spectacle we make of ourselves while we're alive, we might at least try to achieve some dignity when the whole thing's over. Miss Peabody, you can sleep quite easily. Please turn out the light as you leave, it's right there beside the door." Evelyn Peabody stood up. When the room was dark, she said, "And then? And then there's nothing afterwards?"

"Yes, oh yes of course there is," said Mrs. Morris. "A great deal. All eternity. Miss Peabody, you will be amazed."

9 Joe was hosing out the monkey cage. He could see that Linda had come and was waiting by the ticket booth, but he went calmly on with his work and didn't wave. When the cage was finished, he put a new cassette in his tape recorder, turned it up to full volume, and yelled to the cashier, "I'm leaving for half an hour. If any people come, give each of the ladies an hibiscus!" He walked past Linda with the tape recorder in one hand, past the motorcycle standing in its usual place. It was very hot. They walked side by side out onto the pier and he kept the Electric Prune at full volume all the way and let the music hammer his head empty. Walking the whole length of the pier took a hopelessly long time. On the Honda, they would have been there in a minute. Less! Sometimes when there was a wind he rode out—one turn around the embankment to get up speed and then right straight out the whole way, the Honda leaning

into the wind and his body straight as a pole, and then braking and stopping with the front wheel right on the edge, his feet on the asphalt, bam on the nose. Speed was absolute, nothing but itself, pure, like rock. As natural as breathing. Speed, Rock, Jesus. The best things you could give to a person who was willing to receive and understand.

They came to the end and sat down with their legs over the edge. The Electric Prune had worked itself up to a frenzy.

"Do you want mustard or just ketchup?" Linda yelled. She had spread a handkerchief on the asphalt and taken out Coke and hot dogs.

"What'd you say?" Joe screamed. "Talk louder!"

"Mustard! Do you want mustard!" It was just like her. A normal person who didn't like rock would have yelled turn it off, turn it down, it's driving me crazy, but not Linda, no! She suffered in silence and asked if you wanted mustard, and if you took her to a club she listened politely and nodded and smiled encouragingly and was a monument of self-control. A thousand miles away, a thousand years! Like her Mama. Out of reach.

He turned his head and saw that Linda was laughing. Her face was open with delight, and she couldn't stop. She threw her arms around him and screamed, "There isn't any mustard! I forgot it! Isn't that funny?" The Electric Prune had reached the last drum crescendo and Joe yelled that he loved her as loud as he could, and the cassette clicked off so that those three words sailed out into utter silence and became enormous, bigger than the sea. He lay down beside her and whispered that she could have anything she wanted, anything, she could pick whatever she liked from the souvenir shop, as long as it wasn't too big.

"I want to make love," Linda said. "Right now I want to make love."

"But they can see us."

"Of course they can't. We are just two little dots way out at the end. No one can see if the dots are beside each other or on top of each other."

"You talk too much," Joe said. He sat up and looked at their hot dogs lying next to each other on the handkerchief. He felt silly. Linda asked for one with ketchup and stared straight up at the sky as she ate it. "Okay," she said. "Then I'll talk instead. Shall I tell you about Mr. Thompson?"

"No, not Thompson." He knew all about Thompson's box under the bed, his constipation, and his gentle behavior. He knew all about Linda's nice old grannies at the Berkeley Arms. "No hundred-year-olds right now. Something else."

"Then I'll tell you about the music," she said. "They play every evening in the park just before it gets dark, when it's cool and nice. All the mamas come to the bandstand and bring their babies with them and all the lovers come too. The church bells ring and the sky is yellow. The trees are full of black birds."

"You mean in Guadalajara."

"Yes. In Guadalajara."

The distant, well-known name—Guadalajara. The name of his helpless jealousy and Linda's secret life, obedient, back-breaking years with her silent mother while five of her little brothers and sisters died. He knew their names by heart. Five little sugar skulls from Guadalajara.

"They played evening music," Linda said. "The bandstand is very pretty."

Now there was no way out, he would have to listen to the whole unhappy story—her mama who could never come because someone was always sick or dying, and her papa who slept in the arcades, and Linda and Mama who got down on their knees outside on the square with the sick child between them and crawled up the steps of the church and all the way in to the altar. He sighed. "And then you had white balloons," he said.

"No," Linda said. "They were all different colors. The whole top of the church was full of bright colored balloons. A sick child gets to choose his own color. They are only white at the funeral."

"Oh, who cares? Why do we have to talk about all that?"

"But I'm not telling you about the church," Linda said. "I'm telling about the bandstand. Before the music starts all the children run around and chase each other and scream, and their mamas yell at them. The smallest ones nurse. It gets darker and darker and finally they light the lamps." She closed her eyes so she could see the bandstand with its high round roof held up by stone women and adorned with birds. The trees in the park were full of whistling birds that no one could see until they began to look for a place to roost, black birds in black trees. The treetops moved and fluttered with wings against the yellow sky. The marble fountain was as white as snow. Then long sweeping rows of lamps were lit inside the bandstand and they started to play.

"We have to get going," Joe said. "The Tampa bus may be here any minute. And what did they play in that bandstand?"

"Evening music."

"Did she like music?"

"I don't know," Linda said.

"Did she laugh a lot? Did she cry? Did she cry when they died?"

"No."

"Well what did she do? What did she say?"

"She said nothing. What should she say?"

"I can't figure you out," Joe said. "I can't see why you always have to talk about old people and people who are dying all the time, when so many important things are happening right now. I think it's ridiculous. It makes me sad to hear how miserable you were down there."

"But we were happy," said Linda in surprise. "We weren't unhappy." They walked back down the pier and Joe tried to think of something to say but he couldn't come up with anything at all. When they got to the *Bounty*, Linda smiled and waited a little while the way she always did. A moment of politeness while she watched him walk back to the ship.

10 Rebecca Rubinstein always took taxis. She had bad legs and lots of money. Every day she took a cab to the place where she ate, a deserted restaurant beside the main highway leading north, a long way from the Berkeley Arms. Disregarding other people's mealtimes, she ate her own meals obstinately at an hour when the restaurants were empty. Mrs. Rubinstein had noticed that good food became more important to a person as the years went by—a heavy and a simple gratification. At the same time she felt that eating, conscious, pleasurable eating, was a contemptible pastime, an essentially private and intimate function. She had once read of a nomadic people, probably Arabs, who ate only in solitude. With a cloth covering their faces, they gave in to the unesthetic need to eat. Or maybe they turned away from one another, each of them chewing tactfully with his eyes on a private horizon. The picture amused her. The children of Israel had undoubtedly eaten together in a biblical throng and with good appetite. Mrs. Rubinstein was an ardent Zionist, but never discussed the subject with anyone but herself. She therefore carried within her her own Arab, whom she occasionally granted a point. In this case he was allowed to keep his horizon. She justified her dinner by means of imposing punishments on herself. Of all the ugly, clinical, impersonal restaurants in St. Petersburg, she had chosen the worst. She ate only once a day. She had the taxi wait outside. While one dish after another was placed before her in polite silence, while she sat in the empty room and ate, she was acutely aware of the taxi meter ticking off cent after cent, ticking off and tucking away her money. It was an exquisite torment, which at the same time gave the meal a certain air of muted gaiety. When the meat came in she usually thought of Abrascha, automatically recalling the fat, quiet child to whom a mother's love always gave too much to eat. His way of looking at the steaming beef from under lowered eyelids, greedily and spitefully. Eat, my darling, so you'll grow big and strong, bigger and stronger than Mama. As a teenager he became as slim as a gazelle, slim out of spite, and very beautiful. Then he grew fat again. A fat, nervous businessman.

Rebecca Rubinstein attacked her cutlet, and the knife slipped. The meat flew onto the tablecloth, leaving a broad trail of gravy behind it. As quick as a flash she picked up the meat and put it back and tried to clean off the tablecloth and the plate. The waiter had seen nothing. The linen napkin was large and unwieldy and was quickly covered with dripping food, disgustingly brown and sticky. Trembling with distaste, Mrs. Rubinstein held the soiled object under the edge of the table. It had to be hidden somewhere, maybe in the window behind the curtain. She stood up laboriously with the napkin behind her back, and the attentive waiter came hurrying out of his corner. She called to him that she was too hot, she couldn't stand the heat in here, she had to open a window! "I'm sorry," the waiter said, "they don't open. But wait just a moment . . .!" A stream of damp air blew down from the ceiling and lifted the ribbon on Mrs. Rubinstein's hat. She stepped back toward the table and with her free hand she felt for her coat, which was lying across the back of the chair. Now he'll come after me again and want to put my coat around my shoulders and push the chair in under my *tochis*, what a *shmegehgeh* . . .

"Thank you," she said. "That was nice of you." Maybe he hadn't noticed anything. She had stuffed the napkin in under her coat and was holding it there with her elbow. When the waiter went away, Mrs. Rubinstein put the accursed object into her purse and whispered angrily, "*Mechuleh!* A *chazerai*. . ."

Dessert was served, but still she sat motionless, filled to the brim with revulsion. She was terribly tired. Her legs would never carry her all the way out to the taxi. And smoking didn't make them any stronger. It affected her calves. But then it had to affect her someplace.

A motorcycle pulled up outside the restaurant. It was Bounty Joe. He walked up to the counter with a boyish, gliding, loose-jointed gait. As slim as a gazelle. Mrs. Rubinstein made a sudden movement and then sat

still again. Yes, the way he walked, with studied nonchalance, terribly conscious—the young Abrascha entering
a room. They held their heads and shoulders the same
way. He ordered a hamburger and coffee. She watched
him closely. They are decent, thought Rebecca Rubinstein. Behind the nonchalance there is honesty and an
enormous decency. They are ready for anything and prepared to welcome it. They are generous. And afraid.
We are also afraid, but we don't show it, and we don't
open up to anyone. Our bodies no longer express anything. We have to get along entirely with words, nothing but words. Without words we have no charm. The
gazelles left us behind long ago. She moved her plate
over the worst of the gravy spots and called to Bounty
Joe, a light snap of the fingers in the silent room.

"I know you're Bounty Joe," she said. "My name is
Rubinstein. At the Berkeley Arms we set our clocks by
your motorcycle."

"Is that right?" Joe said. His hamburger lay on a
large white bun that was damp with steam, and he covered it with ketchup and ate. He seemed to have decided that she was friendly and concentrated calmly on
his food. What nerve, thought Mrs. Rubinstein. After
all, I am frightening, I am incredible. He doesn't even
ask how I like St. Petersburg. He doesn't try to be polite, he just eats. In fact eating can be a very simple
business, biting and swallowing as naturally as the sea
cuts off a piece of the sand. Why not? To everything
there is a season, and a time to every purpose. That was
nicely put. But what about us? thought Rebecca Rubinstein with sudden bitterness. What's become of us?

What did we do to deserve this wretchedness where everything is ugly? We can't even eat in peace! If his hamburger slides off his plate he won't even ask for a new tablecloth, that's how little it means to him! But we have to be so careful. It's a disgrace for us to spill on ourselves because it's always on account of our false teeth or because we've forgotten our manners! Ha! "I don't want this dessert," she said.

"It's chocolate cake," Joe said. "And it's paid for, isn't it?"

"Yes indeed," said Mrs. Rubinstein and lit a cigarette. "It's all been paid for." She watched carefully the way he ate the dessert. She watched him squeeze ketchup over five slices of bread and eat that too. Sometimes he would glance up and smile quickly with his head on one side, looking just like Abrascha again. Puppies who try to please you and figure out what you want. All I want is to get out of here and get rid of this loathsome rag in my purse . . . The taxi meter outside was ticking quite audibly. It ticked right through the closed window like a clock, stubbornly and urgently.

"That was good," Joe said. "Thank you very much."

"That's my taxi," said Mrs. Rubinstein defiantly. "I've had it waiting for an hour. Maybe two hours! It's inexcusable to take so much of a person's time and to spend so much money needlessly. Isn't it?"

"I don't think so," Joe said. "Money is so unimportant, and time too." He could see the old woman was angry and upset and he added, reassuringly, "They just don't matter."

"Why not?" said Mrs. Rubinstein. When he didn't answer she leaned across the table and repeated it. "Why not? Why don't they matter?"

"Not any more," Joe said, and smiled at her. Rebecca Rubinstein sank back in her chair. Oh yes, of course, nothing mattered any more. That was the way you comforted people who didn't count—not any more.

"Why are you mad at me?" he said. "Did I say something wrong?"

"Don't be naïve," she said. "I'm quite aware of the fact that for me, today, nothing matters terribly. It doesn't interest me, and I have to go. It's late."

Joe had stood up. He stared into her large, immobile face and cried, "But that isn't what I meant at all. I meant that no one has to wait any more, and no one needs any money. Everything's going to be wonderful!"

"I see," said Mrs. Rubinstein. "That is a remarkable statement. Can you explain what you mean?"

Bounty Joe said nothing for a long time, and slowly his face turned red. "Everything's going to be wonderful," he repeated sullenly.

"Balderdash," said Mrs. Rubinstein impatiently. "Where is my coat? I can't imagine what they've done with my coat . . . " This restaurant was impossible. A mess hall. A stinking swill hole. The boy was embarrassed and wanted to say something nice, but she didn't have the strength to deal with him right now. She was exhausted. Rebecca Rubinstein turned off her inquisitive intelligence and made her way to the waiting taxi. Before he closed the door, she said, "You've been very nice, but now I have to be alone. Take care of yourself, Abrascha, and don't let them cheat you." The cab headed back toward the city.

Bounty Joe walked over to his motorcycle and stopped beside it. "I'll take it up to a hundred and twenty. I'll drive faster than shit, I'll drive the damned thing straight to hell! Now I've denied Him again."

11 It was just then, after the death of the Pihalga sisters and before the Spring Ball, that Miss Peabody learned that Tim Tellerton was coming to town. She was at the hairdresser's. Old Mrs. Bovary knew for a fact that the great Broadway star had reserved a room at Friendship's Rest. Miss Peabody was terribly excited. Life really was remarkable. He could have gone anywhere, anyplace at all in the whole vast United States and he was coming to Second Avenue in St. Petersburg! She remembered him as if it had been yesterday. His famous bright blue eyes and the smile that was once loved across an entire continent.

"Catherine!" she called from outside Frey's glass cage. "Tim Tellerton is coming to town. He's going to live at Friendship's! Do you think he'll give a performance at the City Park?"

"Hardly," remarked Mrs. Rubinstein, who was waiting for her rent receipt. "I imagine even the divine Tellerton has been damaged somewhat by the ravages of time. I wouldn't want to cast doubt on his famous virility, but his reasons for visiting St. Petersburg may not be so different from our own." Peabody didn't understand what she meant and turned anxiously to Frey. Miss Frey translated irritably. "He's old, and that's why he's coming to St. Petersburg." They never could get it through their heads that as long as she was in her glass cage she had work to do, and no time for anything else. She was off limits in her glass cage. Asses, thought Mrs. Rubinstein. Simple asses, all of them. And I'm no better. She stubbed out her cigarette and left the vestibule.

"But he's beautiful," said Evelyn Peabody uncertainly. "He's a great artist."

They told her at Friendship's that he was expected on the three o'clock bus. No one knew if they were going to meet him at the bus or if anyone had bought flowers. The heat increased after two o'clock, and the veranda at the Berkeley Arms lay in open sunshine. She sat at one end and Frey at the other.

"Come sit in Pihalga's chair," Frey called. "You can see better from over here." But Peabody didn't want to sit in Pihalga's chair. She paced slowly back and forth across the veranda and watched Frey stringing her beads, the same pattern over and over again. "Why don't you take away their rocking chairs?" she said. "Or are we allowed to change places? It just gets harder if we wait too long. After all, you can't hurt people's feelings."

"And who do you want to sit next to?" Frey said. "It must be awfully hard to decide when you like everyone." Peabody didn't answer. She was confused by the sudden questions, and right now she couldn't remember all the names and places on the veranda. The heat made her tired.

Ten minutes after three a taxi swung around the corner and stopped on the other side of the street outside Friendship's Rest. Frey let her work rest in her lap. They saw the driver unload two trunks and a suitcase. And then Tim Tellerton stepped out of the car. He looked at the house where he was going to live, and walked toward the crowded veranda. Peabody couldn't see his face. Greet him, she thought anxiously. Stand up and meet him and welcome him! Do something! They finally did get to their feet, and for a few moments the veranda was full of confused movement. The driver carried in the baggage, and then everything was the way it had been. The taxi drove away and they all settled down again in their unbroken row in the afternoon shade.

"One more," said Miss Frey, creaking back and forth. She picked up her beads and went on stringing them. Peabody sat down carefully in Mrs. Higgins's chair. Did he know about the Spring Ball? What if they forgot to sign him up? It was only open to members. But of course Tim Tellerton could go anywhere he wanted. It would be an honor for the Senior Club . . . Miss Frey rocked faster and didn't say anything. Her stomach hurt again. She ought to see a doctor, but maybe it would go away . . . In profile against the sunshine, with the wrinkles in her skinny neck and her constantly blinking eyes, she looked like a lizard. Peabody could tell that Frey's silence was a rejection and she looked away, out across the broad street baking in the sun. After a while she remarked sentimentally that they were all like separate worlds, or like boats that passed in the night.

"What?" Frey said.

"Boats. River boats that never meet. Every veranda is separate and alone."

"Well nobody's stopping you," said Frey irritably. "Row on over. Paddle yourself over there and ask him if he'll take you to the ball."

Evelyn Peabody flinched as if she'd been boxed on the ear and looked down at the floor. Frey had said the unforgivable. A very young Miss Peabody could have been badly wounded by having her modesty questioned. For an old Peabody, the insult was twofold—it implied that there was no longer any need for modesty.

Great iron cramps tore at Frey's stomach. "Him and his musical comedies!" she burst out. "And his TV! His Midmorning Matinee for housewives! That was all a long time ago! He got too old and too fat. And he never got married!"

"He lived for his art," said Peabody stiffly.

"Art, shmart," said Frey, leaning forward as if to share a confidence and pressing her hands against her stomach. "People live their own lives in private," she said slowly, "but of course he was always seen in the right places with the right people, he knew how to keep up appearances! I say the right people. It was women, always women—you see what I mean?"

"No!" cried Evelyn Peabody.

"He wasn't so dumb. He couldn't afford a scandal. Housewives are an important audience." Miss Frey was bent double over the terror in her stomach. "But there was talk," she whispered. "There was talk anyway. And you want to know what they said?"

"No!" Peabody burst out. "I don't. I don't want to know!" She stood up and backed away toward the vestibule, step by step, stumbling over the rocking chairs and staring intently at Frey's mouth, which went on talking in the midst of its little wrinkles, a terrible mouth speaking terrible, alien words, and finally she screamed, "Shut up! You're an evil person, and you're stupid, too!" She stood stock still in horror at what she had said.

"So now you know," said Frey slowly. "And now, finally, I know what you think of me."

Mrs. Rubinstein had come out onto the veranda. "Congratulations," she said, looking at Peabody. "You have finally expressed an opinion and found the courage to make an enemy."

"It's true," she said, her lips numb. "It's dreadful but it's true. And you, Mrs. Rubinstein! I have always admired you, but you are a hard and a dangerous woman!"

"Do you think so?" said Rebecca Rubinstein calmly. "That may be. I'm not an especially pleasant person, and neither is Frey. You could have saved your admiration, my dear. What did you expect?" She gave Peabody a little clap on the arm and went back into the vestibule, followed by Frey with her beads rattling like gallstones, and Evelyn Peabody was left alone with her outspoken enmity. She had not said, "Forgive me, it's the heat," or, "Pay no attention, I didn't mean it the way it sounded," or, simply, "I'm sorry." She hadn't said anything. And her conscience was silent. Her perpetually complaining conscience was silent, freed from its torments for one wonderful moment of relief. In this new void, Peabody walked over to the veranda railing and studied Friendship's Rest window by window. Without shyness or anticipation, she wondered whether they had given him a nice room and whether he was feeling lonely.

He was very tired. It had been a mistake to arrive in the middle of the day. He should have taken a night bus— you just rode along through the darkness and slept a little and stopped occasionally for food and rest rooms at nameless bus stations that were all alike, all unreal and impersonal, and people got on and off distantly, like shadows, and you arrived to a taxi, a key, and a bed. It had been a mistake. A stupid professional courtesy, to allow them to arrange the sort of festive reception that usually gave smaller places such a lift. His arrival in St. Petersburg had frightened him. He was frightened by all these old people who got up from their rocking chairs to stare at him and get in his way and introduce themselves all at once and tell him about cheap eating places and leaky hot water faucets and some Spring Ball —and then suddenly they were all in their rocking chairs again, staring straight out into thin air, and he walked into their house alone.

Tim Tellerton loved crowds of people, throngs, swarms, masses of people milling around him full of anticipation and enthusiasm. He understood their confusion and their inability to express themselves. But he didn't understand these old people at all. They rose up like a flock of birds, fluttered a little, and settled back down. It had nothing to do with him. He was an event, but he wasn't Tim Tellerton.

Tellerton was used to adulation. As the years went by, it came to him less often, perhaps, but he always recognized it as a responsibility, a glory, and a natural part of his work. He realized that the need to worship was immensely powerful, and that even in its most help-less and submissive form, this worship made implacable demands. Idolizing someone gave people an obvious, almost cruel, right of ownership. Tim Tellerton's smile, his large friendly attention, was the pretty picture he gave them, the shield he held up before him. But within it there was a secret arm's length that they seldom no-ticed. People remembered his pleasant, warm voice, but not what he said. They had his hopes for another meet-ing, but not his address. In this way Tellerton managed to preserve loyal affection and honest gratitude, while the very numbers of those around him protected the limited space that was his private property.

The room at Friendship's Rest was bright and pleas-antly impersonal. Tim Tellerton took a bath and began the long, slow process of working on his face. There are old faces that have a breathless beauty, shaped by insight. But beauty can also be purely sculptural. Tellerton's bone structure was exquisite. Now, as he slowly massaged his cheeks and the beautiful arch of his brow, his calm returned. He stared into his own bright blue eyes as he worked. Of course he was overweight. He had to choose. To be slim and lose his face, or to keep his face and be fat. To the best of his knowledge, the skeleton altered exclusively by shrinking.

The room he was in seemed too neatly arranged—the smooth lace antimacassars and the regular folds in the curtains, the symmetrical placement of the knick-knacks, the genteel emptiness. Most rooms were like raincoats —protection and nothing more. He lay down on the bed and fell asleep instantly the way his profession had taught him to do, to disappear quickly and completely when exhaustion, anxiety, and opportunity happened to coincide. In his sleep he became even prettier.

Flowers were delivered to him that evening. Pink roses. According to the card, from a certain Miss Peabody—Welcome to St. Petersburg, with admiration. But there was no Peabody at Friendship's Rest, and no one had ever heard of her.

On the morning of the great Spring Ball, Evelyn Peabody woke up late. Her dreams had been light and gentle, and there wasn't a single little offense on her conscience. Curled up in her own warmth, she thought intensely about Miss Frey. With a new, almost playful cruelty, she exposed Frey's face to the strong light of day and saw it for the first time without the least compassion. This face, now utterly naked, was not organically etched by the furrows and lines that are time's expressive script. This text ran every which way, contradictory and irresolute. Still only a rough draft, it would become more distinct in time but could never be improved or rewritten. As Peabody thought about Frey's face, she poisoned her first honorably stated antagonism, but she did it in good faith. In fact she had never disliked Frey, never disliked anyone at all. People were generally easy to please, easy to ignore or to pity, and when you thought about it, they were all of them fine in their own way. It is possible, thought Evelyn Peabody on the threshold of sleep, it is possible that I never really liked them very much, either, but who among them has ever noticed how hard I try to be fair and true? Who has measured the price of my compassion? She couldn't remember what Frey had said and why she'd been so angry . . . It was nice to go back to sleep.

At twelve o'clock, Frey came up and knocked on the door. "Are you sick in there?" she shouted.

"I'm sleeping," Peabody said. Frey started back downstairs. It was part of the job to keep track of them and where they were. Her stomach felt normal again. Maybe she didn't need to go to the doctor after all. You never knew what he'd find, and anyway she didn't have the time. Peabody indeed. Little Miss Sleeping Beauty with the tender heart. As Frey came down the stairs and around the corner, Thompson rushed out of his room and screamed, "Boo, you old witch!" right in her ear. "You ought to be ashamed!" Frey cried and ran into her glass cage and slammed the door behind her. She tilted back her head and blinked rapidly so her eye liner wouldn't run. "How childish," she whispered. "How awfully childish. How awful." And she let her whole face fall, all the lines of exhaustion and disappointment deepened all at once, all the lines from her eyes and her nose and the corners of her mouth. She was out of tissues. Also, they needed soap, and more brochures, and

Frey sat down at her desk to make a note: brochures, soap. But her pen just made tiny, vague lines, and after a while she realized she was drawing Thompson's hair. She gave him eyebrows and a crooked, triangular face, very close-set eyes and a gaping, black mouth. Finally she gave him big horns, one on each side, and then she wadded the paper into a ball and ran out into the vestibule. "Linda!" she screamed. "Air out his room. The whole house stinks of garlic and tobacco! Why should his room be such a pigsty?"

"Yes, Miss Frey," Linda said and looked at her the way you might look at a strange, nervous animal that hadn't been properly cared for. Frey went upstairs to Room Five. "Mrs. Higgins," she shouted, "are you there? Are you in there? Was it the bed lamp that burned out, or the bulb in the ceiling? I can't speak to Johanson until I know which one is out!"

"It's the bed lamp," said Mrs. Higgins in surprise. "But I think both bulbs are the same." She waited for a moment and looked at Miss Frey. "Now you're all upset again, aren't you? Is it Thompson who's been mean?"

"He's a fiend," Frey said.

"That's a pretty strong word for a childish old man."

"Childish!" said Catherine Frey, and began to tremble. "He's no more childish than Peabody's angelic!" Yes, that was true, the devil could be a child with all its hereditary evil and his angels could hide behind all the virtues in the world . . . She said it again. "A fiend."

"Now, now," said Mrs. Higgins. "Is that so." She very carefully unscrewed the burned-out bulb by the bed. "I've always found it hard to believe in the devil,"

she said. "Angels are easier to picture. I can't understand why Pastor Grimley's sermons are so infernally
dull. I mean, he's an educated man, isn't he?"

"Yes," said Miss Frey weakly and sat down in a chair.
Hannah Higgins went on about Grimley and the Spring
Ball and brought out her beaded jet handbag. "My
grandson the sailor," she said. "He's got taste." Miss Frey
turned and twisted the glittering handbag, blinking her
eyes rapidly. She listened to Mrs. Higgins poke around
in the bathroom and then come back in again still talking about the ball. "Now Catherine, don't wear slacks,
wear something pretty and feminine, and don't wear
your wig. Take off your wig, dear, and let's see what
your own hair looks like." Catherine Frey took off her
wig. Mrs. Higgins studied her for a long time through
her thick glasses, from above and below and one side,
and finally she said that this called for the assistance of a
hairdresser, and quickly too.

The streets of St. Petersburg lay empty in the afternoon heat. Hundreds of old ladies sat under their dryers, while those whose hair was already done awaited the
evening at home. Catherine Frey hurried through the
city, up one street and down the next, and everywhere
they were full. She got flustered and began picking
streets at random and going into salons where she had
been before, but no matter where she went, the dryers
droned on inexorably occupied and everywhere long
rows of women with appointments waited patiently. So
much old hair being washed and set, dyed, sprayed, and
back-combed, so much white and gray down being
brushed up across balding heads! She dashed from one

beauty parlor to another and was continually turned down, but gradually Miss Frey began to forget her troubles and to be overwhelmed by this secret obsession, the magic with which womanhood endowed the care of its own hair, and she was seized by a fabulous calm. Finally she found asylum, far from the Berkeley Arms. She conferred with the hairdresser in hasty, earnest whispers and sank under plastic shrouds deep into a world of damp terrycloth and the humming greenhouse warmth of dryers, a world promising forgetfulness for several peaceful hours. Everything in the crowded room was pink, even the telephone. It was a closed, feminine sanctuary where Miss Frey fell asleep, massaged at last with Silver Spray Number Five.

The last ladies hurried home with their hairdos protected by light silk scarves. The city fell completely silent. Linda had laid out a cold supper in the TV room, paper cartons of chicken and potato salad from the Garden. Everything seemed different, makeshift and rushed like just before a trip. Johanson was to bring the van around in half an hour. Hannah Higgins and Peabody sat across from each other with their party handbags beside them on the table. Mrs. Higgins could see clearly that Peabody was nervous. She would glance at the door and then at the TV, and she kept shifting around all the time. And chicken was not a good idea when a person was nervous before a party. It was an impractical food that could do great damage to a person's clothes.

Then Catherine Frey arrived, in a rustle of taffeta, and Mrs. Higgins put down her fork and said, "Let's have a look at your own hair. Come over here, dear, and turn around . . . Very pretty, silver gray!" Peabody laughed, a short yelp that wasn't friendly, and Frey walked over to the TV as if she'd been bitten by a snake and stood and watched it with her back to them. It was about a lumberjack in the Northwest. He answered only yes and no and looked cross.

"Just like a picnic," Peabody said. "It's such fun to eat out of paper cartons."

"Hush!" Frey hissed. "We're watching the program!" But Peabody went right on in a loud voice about what a wonderful thing the ball was, and had anyone seen Mrs. Rubinstein's hat? But of course that was always supposed to be such a surprise.

"Why are you talking so unnaturally?" asked Hannah Higgins. "Have you had a quarrel?"

"Hush!" said Frey once more. She walked up close to the screen to show how much they were disturbing her. "The trees are so huge!" she cried. "You can drive right through them in a car! Look at them, look!"But when they looked there was nothing to see but the surly face of the lumberjack, until he was blanked out by a commercial.

"Yes," said Hannah Higgins, "it certainly would be fun to see a tree that big, and even drive right through it . . . "

"Oh nonsense!" Peabody burst out, and threw herself back in the sofa.

"Eat your food," said Mrs. Higgins sternly. "The world is larger than you think." It was already dusk in the room. The cool of the evening came in through the open window. They heard the van drive up in front of the veranda. Miss Frey walked quickly past them out into the vestibule, and Peabody whispered, "Poor woman."

"Save your breath," said Hannah Higgins. "Rash words are like dry leaves in the wind. To feel sorry you have to understand, and if you understand someone you have to like them."

"No, no," whispered Evelyn Peabody nervously. "Everything is changed. We're enemies!" Mrs. Higgins heaved a little sigh and observed that people could be many different things, so long as they knew what they wanted. She picked up her handbag and left the room. Out on the street, people in evening clothes were making their way toward the harbor, in groups or two by two. All the dresses were long, and bright in the twilight. They stood out boldly against the greenery surrounding the houses. Several cars drove down Second Avenue toward the bay and the Senior Club.

Mrs. Morris had dressed for the Ball absent-mindedly but still with care. Now she sat by the open window and watched the people and the cars, the stream of anticipation moving toward the brightly lit ship, and she felt an irresistable desire simply to stay home and be by herself. This sudden new inclination gave Mrs. Morris a feeling of gaiety and personal freedom. She straightened up in her chair and slowly pulled on one of her long blue gloves. Peabody scratched at the door and asked if she was ready and if she'd remembered to join the Senior Club. "Yes," said Mrs. Morris. "Don't worry.

Everything's just fine." And Miss Peabody bounded down the stairs and out onto the street, which was empty. Johanson had driven away. She ran a few steps out into the street and then back again. Hunched up under her gray shawl, she looked more than ever like a mouse—sniffing the air, always in flight, constantly dashing out of some new hole. Thompson limped by her on his way up the street toward Palmer's. He was wearing his black suit and a strange hat. Mrs. Morris heard him say, "Hurry up, Peabody. We've got time for a beer before it starts. Grandpa Johanson will have to manage his holy chariot without us."

The bar was changed, brightly lit and full of people trying to drown out the music. It frightened her, and she stopped in the doorway. "Peabody!" Thompson shouted. "Come on in and sit down!" He drove his left elbow into the man beside him and managed to get him off his stool. It was very embarrassing and hard to climb up with a long skirt, and she tried to apologize. "Excuse me, this was your stool." But the big man didn't hear what she said. He leaned across the bar and hollered, "Hey! A Planter's Punch for grannie here!" A big glass came sailing down the bar. He winked respectfully and said, "How's it going with little Aloha? Did he hear from the Jesus people?"

Thompson sat very still, as if he'd been in church. In the strong light he looked surprisingly small and very dusty. Peabody explained that she didn't know Bounty Joe personally, but no one was listening. Out of politeness she drank the large glass first and then the beer, and she rested her arms on the bar, which felt so nice for her back. In here everyone was friends. They all talked at once in an enthusiastic frenzy and couldn't agree on anything. All down the long bar she could see explaining and protesting hands, profiles and the backs of heads, a swarm of movement, men who hung over the bar and then threw themselves backward in laughter, their necks outstretched. Sometimes one of them would go to the jukebox and play more music. Palmer's, she knew, was a place where people went to calm their nerves. She stuck a five dollar bill under Thompson's arm, and he ordered two more beers. The room felt like absolute security, inexplicable but persuasive. Why, thought Peabody, why can't they just let me be nice? I'm such an unusually nice person. Evelyn Peabody lost herself in the mirror behind the bar, where she regarded her own compassion, her upright honesty that occasionally threw out long needles of hate, like thorns on a rose. How is it possible? thought Peabody with a twinge of pain. What is happening to me? None of them has such a bad conscience as I do, none of them cares as much as I do. I am crushed to the earth by my conscience, yes, I'm crushed to the earth. And I can't even have the tiniest little enemy all to myself in peace.

"Hey Peabody," Thompson said. "Are you asleep?" All of a sudden the bar grew empty as one after the other the customers paid and left.

"Why are they all leaving?" asked Peabody nervously.

"They're going home to eat."

"Aren't they coming back?"

"They're coming back," Thompson said. "They're all coming back sooner or later. Don't worry about it."

The street was very quiet and empty, like coming out of a movie. Everything seemed wrong. They walked toward the bay. He told her that when you got right down to it, Palmer's wasn't really all that hot. Now the bars in San Francisco, she ought to see them! The wind was blowing a cool steady breeze. They walked two blocks and then Peabody mentioned the Cavalcade of Hats and Mrs. Rubinstein.

"Peabody," said Thompson, "what are you talking about? Are you talking about hats?"

"Yes," she said uneasily.

"Hats! A lot of hats on a bunch of big stupid women —what a sight! A sight I've seen way too often!"

"Of course," said Peabody wisely. "It's so cold up north. Do you mean the hats or the women?"

"Both," he said. "Be quiet, Peabody." They walked slowly on down the empty avenue toward the brightly lit rigging of the *Bounty*.

When Mrs. Rubinstein was fully dressed she went to Miss Ruthermer-Berkeley's room to show her her hat. They seldom met, but entertained a distant and fascinated respect for one another. Every year, just before the Spring Ball, they would have a little conference. The crystal chandelier and the sconces were lit; Mrs. Rubinstein was expected. Conscious of the pleasure her entrance could afford, she stopped for a moment in the door to be admired. This year, the huge, majestic woman was dressed in black paillettes, a glittering mantle of anachronistic spangles that followed the curves of her body from a white décolletage down over powerful arms and a muscular stomach toward the floor, where it spread out in a sweeping, rustling train. With one hand Mrs. Rubinstein steadied herself against the doorpost, and with the other she reached up and gently touched the enormous, overshadowing hat. This year it was red, dark red silk with violet roses, some of them surprisingly blue. One blue rose had been permitted to fall down over her left eye. The right eye stared out black and triumphant, calculating.

"Mrs. Rubinstein, you are magnificent," said Miss Ruthermer-Berkeley. "May I offer you a glass of sherry?" The crystal carafe stood on the oval table with two waiting glasses. Mrs. Rubinstein served both of them and expressed her considered opinion that the traditions of the Senior Club needed revision. As long as she was on the board she had tried her best, but had been outmaneuvered before she could accomplish very much. "You were probably too domineering," Miss Ruthermer-Berkeley said. "Old people are creatures of habit, it can't be helped. Perhaps you'd like a cigarette?" Mrs. Rubinstein declined politely. "I know," she said. "I scare them. It's hard to keep from being overbearing when you can see quite clearly what ought to be changed, and how it could be done. Suppose someone is trying to move a heavy object up a hill, using leverage, say, and you can see that the balance is wrong. It is very hard not to run up and tell them where to apply their leverage so as to achieve the desired effect and avoid

catastrophe. People know so extremely little about organization." Miss Ruthermer-Berkeley was listening at-
tentively. "That's true," she said. "I might add, in that
connection, that for a long time I have toyed with the
notion that you, Mrs. Rubinstein, might be just the person to modernize the Berkeley Arms and give the house
a new vitality and purpose. Unfortunately, it is only a
notion. Promises and loyalty are important things, and
competence must sometimes take the place of creative
imagination."

"She's tired," said Mrs. Rubinstein quickly, without
thinking.

"Yes, right at the moment she is tired. But she'll pull
herself together in a few years, when she reaches the age
where a person gets new ideas and abandons the old
ones that no longer work. The only right and just thing
is to wait and see. Mrs. Rubinstein, I wish you the best
of luck in the Cavalcade of Hats. It would not surprise
me if once again you brought home the green ribbon to
the Berkeley Arms." She raised her untouched glass to
her lips and they parted for the evening. Outside the
door, Mrs. Rubinstein lit a cigarette and thought,
Tired? Ha! I was never tired at Frey's age, never. Frey
was born without vitality, and getting old won't give
her any.

Linda called a taxi and Mrs. Rubinstein arrived at
the Senior Club at precisely the right moment. The
Cavalcade stood waiting for the music to begin. Someone held the door and she walked slowly into the ballroom, across the floor, and took her place at the head of
a line of ladies in wonderful hats.

12 By the time Peabody and Thompson arrived, there were only a few people left in the lobby—the timid souls and the late-comers and a couple of confused ladies from Las Olas. Thompson searched for his wallet until Peabody had fished out a five dollar bill, and they both had their cards stamped at the ballroom door. Miss Frey hurried past them. She was always in a hurry, as if she were late for an appointment or rushing to prevent some terrible disaster. Thompson observed that old girls with new faces were a depressing sight although they looked just the way they did before, and suddenly he felt sad. They were playing a slow waltz. The ball always opened with a lively number and then the music would grow steadily calmer until as midnight approached they played nothing but very gentle blues. The cotillion, of course, was the great exception. It was played as it would have been at the turn of the century. Thompson held on to Pea-

body's dress and they tried to make their way to benches
but immediately got caught in a crowd of dancing,
jostling people. They forced their way into a window
alcove where things were comparatively quiet, and
Thompson sank into his veranda silence. Across from
them the room was full of women sitting on row after
row of wooden benches all the way back to the wall.
Rotating spotlights lit them up at regular intervals like
beacons. The Cavalcade of Hats was over, and the enormous, homemade hats lay on the stage in front of the
orchestra, each one prettier than the one before—flower
gardens and wedding cakes, irrepressibly romantic. Mrs.
Rubinstein was dancing with the Mayor. She was wearing a green ribbon across her bosom.

"She's won first prize again!" Peabody shouted in
Thompson's ear. But he wasn't listening; he was inaccessible, sheltered by his contempt. No one else from the
Berkeley Arms was out on the floor, only the fantastic
Mrs. Rubinstein. Evelyn Peabody was proud of her and
tears came to her eyes the same way they always did at
the raising of the stars and stripes. A Spring Ball was a
wonderful thing. All the ladies were dressed to the nines
with plumes and swan's-down fluttering as they waltzed,
like summer meadows. Oh, such attention to beauty.
Many of them had fastened delicate scarves to their
wrists, and these scarves marked the rhythm of the dance
in long, sweeping arabesques, around and around in all
the colors of the rainbow. These women had lavished
the feminine experience of a lifetime on the Spring
Ball, everything they had ever learned about the seduc-
tion of the eye. The gentlemen held the ladies' wrinkled

backs and puffed their way around the floor, most of them in suit and tie. Between the windows hung the board's warning in large, clear letters: MEMBERS DANCE AT THEIR OWN RISK. But the nurse out in the lobby wore street clothes—that much at least Mrs. Rubinstein had accomplished before they forced her off the board. She listened carefully to the Mayor's breathing and suggested a cigarette in the lobby after their first circuit of the room. Anyway, she wasn't the least bit interested in dancing. It was very warm. The vast, long ballroom was fermenting a peculiar smell, stale and sweet, but the windows could not be opened because of the draft. Mrs. Rubinstein drew deeply on her cigarette and peered at the Mayor through the smoke. He was much shorter than she was and he seemed preoccupied. "I have an idea," she said. "A little present to the board. Why not divide up the space according to the members' health? One ballroom for those who can't take air and another for those who can't take smoke? One ballroom with slow tangos and dim lighting for the ones with bad hearts and wrinkled décolletage, and another one with fluorescent lights and pop music for the ones with poor eyesight and hearing?"

"You will have your little joke," said the Mayor without smiling. Maybe he'd be able to get out of here and go home by nine o'clock without attracting attention. But that was probably hoping for too much. The cashier came up to them and said, "Excuse me, Madame, but you forgot to pay the entrance fee. That will be two dollars." Mrs. Rubinstein was suddenly furious.

"I'll send it over tomorrow with the chauffeur," she said. Her train rustled as she swung around and walked out of the fluorescent lighting, through the café to the back yard on the bay. She stood there and waited until her heart calmed down.

"I'm going out for a while," Peabody said, a little louder this time, but Thompson had disappeared deep into his most unapproachable sanctuary and didn't answer.

Tim Tellerton had not come—he was nowhere to be seen. No one had told him about the Spring Ball. Someone had to call him, it still wasn't too late. This is the Senior Club calling. We're having a little dance. We heard you were visiting St. Petersburg, and it would be a great honor . . . She wouldn't have to give her name, just say it was the Senior Club. Very agitated, Peabody began looking for her reading glasses and remembered that she'd left them in her other purse. She carried the phone book to the cashier and said please, she wanted to call Friendship's Rest, a very important call, but her glasses were at home, these were only for distance. The cashier looked it up. "643-1621," she said.

"I'm afraid I don't have a pen either," Peabody said. "Do you think you could write it down for me, too?"

"I haven't got a pencil," the girl said. "643-1621."

"641-6321?" The cashier walked to the phone and dialed the number. "There you go," she said, and went back to her table. But the line was busy. Peabody hung up the phone.

The music stopped and a lot of people came out in the lobby to smoke. Frey hurried by looking the other way. Two men stood nearby talking about the dog races. One of them had a fountain pen in his breast pocket.

"Excuse me," Peabody said, "but could I borrow your pen for just a moment?"

"Beg pardon? I didn't hear what you said," said the man with the pen.

"Could I possibly borrow your fountain pen?"

"But I'm afraid I don't have a fountain pen."

"There!" said Peabody desperately. "In your pocket!"

"That's a cigar," he said. "I'm sorry." She went back to Thompson's alcove and sat down beside him with her hands in her lap. A few moments later, Thompson started to snore. He fell slowly to one side and then straightened up with a jerk. His necktie was crooked. And in the inside pocket of his jacket, Peabody could see a very small, black ballpoint pen.

She tried to speak softly, matter-of-factly, as impersonally as she could. It was very nice of them, said Tim Tellerton in his lovely professional voice. The Senior Club, across from the *Bounty*. He was used to getting names quickly and remembering them—it was part of his job. "I am very grateful for the invitation, which I will be happy to accept at a later date."

"No, no," Peabody whispered. She had been prepared for all sorts of difficulties but not a refusal.

"Hello?" he said. "Are you there?"

"Yes," she said.

There was a long silence. "With whom do I have the honor of speaking?" he asked finally.

"Peabody. Miss Peabody."

"Miss Peabody. Then I can thank you at last for the lovely flowers. Your thoughtfulness was much appreciated."

Someone was standing beside her waiting to use the phone. She pressed the receiver close to her lips. "It was nothing," she breathed, "nothing at all . . . "

"Miss Peabody, I hope we will have a chance to meet."

"Yes," she answered blindly, "that would be very easy. All you have to do is take a taxi. This is the only ball all spring, and it would be a shame . . . I mean, we would be so disappointed, we've prepared a little reception . . . "

"How very kind," said Tim Tellerton coolly. "I'll see what I can do."

Peabody hung up the receiver and was seized by panic. She had been telling fibs again. There wasn't any reception or any flowers or anything. She hurried over to the cashier and explained that they were going to have a guest of honor, my dear girl, a guest of honor —Tim Tellerton!

"Who?"

"Tim Tellerton, the great singing star!"

"Never heard of him," the girl said.

"I know, of course not," Peabody said. "You're too young. You couldn't possibly have heard of him, it's perfectly natural. But he is very famous and he's going to be here any moment. Here's two dollars for his entrance fee, and he can sign up later, can't he?"

"No, I don't think so," the cashier said. "He has to be a member, and that has to go through the office."

"But my dear girl, he's on his way! He's famous!"

"I'm awfully sorry," the girl said, "but I have orders from the board."

The orchestra started to play again, and the lobby emptied. Only Mrs. Rubinstein was left, standing in the door to the café. Her large face was very white. "What's this all about?" she said. "Miss Peabody?"

Peabody hurried over to her. "You don't know," she whispered urgently, "you don't know what's happened! Tim Tellerton is coming. He might be here any moment and we haven't prepared a welcome for him and they won't even let him in without a membership card!"

Mrs. Rubinstein gestured impatiently. "Give me facts," she said. "As briefly as you can. You asked him to come?"

"Yes."

"On your own, or on behalf of the club?"

"On behalf of the club," Peabody whispered.

"Is there anything else I need to know?"

"I sent him some roses, and he's annoyed, and I said we'd prepared a reception!"

Mrs. Rubinstein turned to the cashier. "My dear," she said, "you will not make any difficulties when Mr. Tellerton arrives. He was invited by the board." She walked into the ballroom and signaled to the orchestra leader. "Mr. Ogden, we're going to have a guest of honor. Please watch closely. When you see me in the doorway with an elderly, rather stout gentleman, stop the music. Play a fanfare and then go right into 'Tim's Twinkle.' Is that clear?"

"I'm afraid I don't know it," Mr. Ogden said.

"In that case, just play the fanfare. Someone in the orchestra can hand me my hat, the one closest to the door, and then play a slow waltz, just once around."

"Okay," said Mr. Ogden. "But don't bring him in until we're done with the twenties—she's waiting backstage." Mrs. Rubinstein nodded and went out to the street. Near the entrance stood a flock of leather jackets, more slender young men with lots of hair. She took a step toward them. "Good evening," she said. "I need your help." They swung around to look at her; one of them was Bounty Joe. "In a little while," she went on, "an old man will arrive in a taxi. He was once a great vaudeville star and his name is Tim Tellerton. Tim Tellerton. I would like you to put on a display of enthusiasm when he arrives."

She's like the figurehead on a ship, Joe thought. A big one. She's bigger than she was last time. He walked up to her. "All right, Mrs. Rubinstein," he said. "We'll take care of it." The group behind him didn't move; their cigarettes glowed motionlessly in their hands. They stared at her the way people stare at a creature from another world. "Joe," said Mrs. Rubinstein. She paused for a moment but couldn't think of anything to add, and walked back to the Senior Club.

Mr. Ogden was standing at the footlights with his arms outstretched. "The Twenties!" he called out.

"Come with us to the irresistible Twenties! Let yourselves be carried back, let yourselves remember, let each
of us return for a moment to his or her own . . . fabulous
. . . Twenties!" He raised his voice. "And let us all
welcome Miss . . . Alicia . . . Brown!" And out she came,
for the hundredth time, bubbling with playfulness and
stage fright, wearing black acetate, what a surprise, it
used to be called satin and was shinier and cheaper, with
a long cigarette holder in one hand and the other at her
skinny, sagging waist. Stiffly, but like the veteran she
was, she strutted to the center of the stage and began to
sing: The dolphin, the koala, and little miss mouse,
playing poker in the kitchen at koala's house, they were
two of them flush and they were two of them free, they
were three of a kind on a whee of a spree. Not bad, she
knew her stuff. She still had style. Nearly seventy. Her
legs had grown thin in the wrong places, but they were
all right as long as she didn't move them. The spotlight
lit her from almost directly overhead and spared her
throat. Her face was still heart-shaped, and was decorated with astonished eyebrows. The dolphin and koala
said they'd play all night, they were ready to bet if she
was ready to bite. Now miss mouse was ready for a warm
little bed, but she played poker with koala and the dolphin instead. Hannah Higgins sat amidships in the rows
of benches, nodding in time to the music and remembering each happy new innocent verse. They certainly
are polite to us, she thought. The Twenties was much
later. Although of course it would be fun if she'd sing a
song from the days when we really were young and people's clothes were pretty. The dolphin was dealing but

little miss mouse said she had to go home to her own little house . . . And then the orchestra went on alone and Miss Alicia Brown became a black and white photograph, captured, immobile, as she stared into the darkness of the ballroom.

"Poor dear," said Mrs. Higgins. "She's forgotten the words." And Mrs. Rubinstein thought: Aphasia. Blackout. Mr. Ogden took it again from The dolphin was dealing, but Miss Brown was still silent. She raised her hands and covered her face, an attitude of shame, and then she spread her arms wide in disarming assurance of forgiveness. The forgiveness came instantly, a terrific burst of applause. St. Petersburg loved Miss Alicia Brown and understood her perfectly. Mr. Ogden took it from the top, but this time slowly, much more slowly. The dolphin and the koala and little miss mouse came toward them almost like characters in a romance, and everyone sang along, over and over again they sang the first two verses with Miss Alicia Brown. Ogden was no fool—he knew his business.

All his life, Tim Tellerton had been fascinated by women older than himself, women who could give pleasure to the eye and provide intelligent companionship without extremes. He thought highly of the kind of friendship that was unsullied by the misfortune of exaggerated intimacy but that managed nevertheless to retain a spark of excitement, an implied significance that was never enunciated. There were very few women who could savor and preserve this elegant distance for any length of time. They seldom had the necessary sense of subtlety and balance. Little by little they allowed age to obliterate both femininity and pride, especially the pride of being old, the dignified knowledge of how to grow old gracefully that was granted to a queen.

The veranda at Friendship's Rest had frightened him. The whole city was disquieting. The sight of a fragile, white-haired lady had always aroused strong, beautiful emotions in Tim Tellerton, but the sight of hundreds of them made him uncomfortable. As he changed his clothes, he decided that Miss Peabody was one more of those women who had failed to achieve the refinement of age. His own compliance was merely a tribute to the good breeding he had never betrayed.

Florida's famous moon had risen and hovered over the *Bounty* in its perfection. The taxi driver said it was hot for that time of year. Next year he was going to join Senior's himself. He liked to play bridge.

"An intelligent game," Tellerton replied.

The pier lay in blue moonlight, and when the cab stopped a group of young people came slowly toward them, shouting something he couldn't make out. The driver threw open the door and shouted, "You kids get out of here and don't make any trouble!" In a singsong chant they began to call his name, "Tim Tellerton Tim, Tim Tellerton Tim," stamping their feet in time. One of them crouched on the asphalt and handed him a flower. They're hippies, he thought. They're friendly, they know who I am. He climbed out of the car and turned toward them and tried desperately to find words, words for hippies . . . Holding the flower in one hand, he shouted, "Love! What a beautiful night!" They replied with a roar, a long drawn-out howl. And then a huge woman came toward him, Mrs. Rubinstein, on behalf of the club, and he was led into a dreary room that smelled bad and the orchestra played a fanfare. A moment later the woman beside him was wearing an enormous hat. He danced a slow waltz through a sea of old people who changed color from red to green and green to red. The hat was in his way, and he was still holding the flower in one hand. Beneath his closed fist he could feel a strong back and the edges of hard spangles. "Your invitation was a great honor," he said.

"I know the hat is a nuisance," replied Mrs. Rubinstein. "Once around and I can take it off. It's a tradition I have to maintain."

"It's important to maintain old traditions," mumbled Tellerton automatically. At the same time he let her know with a smile that he had grasped their professional responsibility. They danced on in silence. When the music stopped, he put the flower in his pocket. It was large and damp, probably an hibiscus. "And now," he said, "I would appreciate it if you could introduce me to a certain Miss Peabody." But Peabody wasn't there. She had gone out to the parking lot.

From where she stood among the parked cars she could see the pack of boys wandering on out the pier, slowly and mournfully singing, "Tim Tellerton Tim, Tim Tellerton Tim." It sounded like a hymn. They were moving in a sort of half dance, and all of a sudden she heard them burst out laughing.

"Oh there you are, Peabody," Thompson said. "What a godawful party. Have a little cognac."

"No thanks, I'm depressed. I behaved badly."

"All the more reason. Peabody, you're hopeless. And you never learn."

The cognac helped. The boys started to sing again, and the song turned into a howl, and they started to dance—a parody of the gentle music streaming out of the Senior Club along with the light. They were moving very slowly, as if in an incantation or a rite. Thompson sat down on the ground with one hand in his hair. He tried to say something, but Peabody wasn't listening. She was staring at the boys dancing in the moonlight, their slim legs carrying them farther and farther out on the pier, dancing solemnly over their shadows, and suddenly these young creatures seemed threatening and fateful. In an irrational moment she got the idea that they were harbingers of death, that they were like death itself, relentless, imcomprehensible, and beautiful, and she shared her insight with Thompson. "Death is young," she said. "He is very young."

"Peabody," said Thompson, "you're pretty mixed up, but it doesn't matter. Now pull yourself together. We were talking about San Francisco. It's a hard city. That's where my friend lives, a very wise man named Jeremiah Spennert. Are you listening? We used to sit around talking in the evenings, and the light was so dim that all you could see was his teeth."

"Why was that?" asked Peabody with her thoughts far away.

"The lights. I said the lighting was bad. He was uncommonly smart, that man."

"But of course," she said. "I don't see why not."

"Black!" Thompson shouted. "Jeremiah Spennert is coal black. Peabody, why don't you ever listen to what I'm saying?"

Bounty Joe started his motorcycle and drove back and forth across the pier in great figure eights, then roared past them up toward town. She saw only the white cross he had painted on the back of the mudguard with phosphorescent paint.

"Dear Jesus," Peabody said. "The sign of death."

Everyone still at home at the Berkeley Arms had turned out their lights and gone to bed, and the greenery in the back yard lay in darkness. Only the flowers on the bushes glowed white. It was an anonymous and sheltered place. Elizabeth Morris walked slowly back and forth across the grass. Sometimes she stood still and listened for the wind from the ocean, hardly more than a breath of air.

"Good evening, Mrs. Morris," said Linda, standing in the black square of her window, her face like a flower in the darkness.

"This is a lovely place," Elizabeth Morris said. "It smells so good." They heard the motorcycle start down by the harbor and drive up the avenue past the City Park. "Mrs. Morris," said Linda when it was quiet again, "may I speak about his Honda? May I ask you if you like machines?"

"Not particularly."

"He loves it," Linda said. "He loves it like a baby. He saved for it since he was thirteen years old. Mrs. Morris, you're not in a hurry? It can go 120 miles an hour. It takes the curves like an angel. What shall I do? He wants me to come with him on the Honda to Silver Springs."

"Are you afraid?" Mrs. Morris asked.

"Of what?"

"Of having an accident, of getting killed," said Elizabeth Morris and walked on across the grass and right up to the bushes until the leaves touched her face. Linda laughed behind her. "I won't die," came her pleasant voice. "It's only that I hate machines. And my mama hates them. And all real women hate them."

There was probably more of a breeze down at the pier. The heat had been exhausting. "What is it you want?" she said. "What do you know about real women? He likes his motorcycle and you like him. Nothing could be simpler. You accept his motorcycle."

"Yes, Mrs. Morris."

"Why do you ask me things you already know?"

"I don't know," Linda said. "Good night, Mrs. Morris!"

Out on the street, the wind was a cool, even current. She walked very slowly down toward the harbor, enjoying the beautiful night. The pier was empty. The fluorescent light from inside the Senior Club reached far out onto the asphalt through the open front door, and she stopped for a moment to look into the lobby, where the cashier sat reading at her table. It was a dreary, paneled room, hardly more than a barracks. Mrs. Morris turned to go home. How dumb, she thought. How awful. That they couldn't give the threshold to their great expectation the least little festive air. I'll bet they have to hang their mink coats on a nail. I know there isn't even a single mirror.

Two old women emerged from the lobby. They stood tall and straight and wore tiaras in their white hair. Standing there beside each other in their long dresses, their faces turned to the wind, they looked like two queens indulging in a moment of solitude. They returned to the Senior Club side by side, and their manner of passing through the dismal room stripped its nakedness of all meaning and removed all doubt but what the Spring Ball was a dignified and glittering celebration.

Mrs. Morris paid the cashier and showed her membership card. The card was stamped at the door to the ballroom and she was enjoined to refrain from smoking. The ballroom was bathed in pink light. A feeling of excitement and great anxiety came toward her like a wave. Suddenly Miss Frey was standing right beside her. "Cotillion!" she whispered. "That's the Chief Surgeon from Greenwood calling out the couples . . . "

The Chief Surgeon was standing in front of the stage calling out the couples for St. Petersburg's great annual Cotillion. He had done this at every Spring Ball for fifteen years, and before him it had been the Chief of Internal Medicine. On either side of him, stiff as posts, stood the gentlemen of the ball, each one bearing the colors of his unknown lady. "White pennant!" called the Chief Surgeon. And in the silence, embarrassed and self-conscious, a lady in party finery would separate herself from the sea of expectant women and steal across the floor toward the gentleman who wore the white pennant, take her place beside him, and stare off into space. "What are they doing?" Mrs. Morris asked. "What's going on?" Catherine Frey answered without taking her eyes from the stage. "It's the luck of the draw. Anyone who wants to can dance, but you have to get here early— there aren't all that many colors . . . This year those ladies came an hour ahead of time and got them all!"

"Green star!" called the Chief Surgeon from Greenwood Hospital. "Yellow rose! Red and blue bow!" And finally the colors were gone and the Cotillion velvet tray was empty. Pair by pair, the chosen dancers waited for the music. They didn't look at each other. The spotlights began to revolve in orange and dark red. The orchestra struck up the Cotillion. The white pennant danced out with the white pennant, the yellow rose with the yellow rose. St. Petersburg's annual Cotillion was very old. It was characterized by a festive gravity, and by melodic specifications that always aroused sorrowful but pleasant shivers of recognition and memory. The long, tight rows of extra women sat in silence, watching the dancers intently. Tim Tellerton bent over an incredibly tiny, stiff-legged lady and tried to carry her with him through the turns. She was breathing heavily.

"Elizabeth!" shouted Mrs. Higgins and stood up in the middle of a row. "Elizabeth, I want to dance!" It was hard to get out past all the knees, but with apologies to left and right she finally made her way to the dance floor and gave Mrs. Morris her hand.

"Mrs. Higgins, dear," said Mrs. Rubinstein quickly, "I don't think you'd better. My proposal for a ladies' dance was put before the board but voted down."

"Don't worry, Rebecca," said Mrs. Higgins. "Where I come from we used to dance with each other all the time." They listened for a moment, gravely, and moved off into the leisurely waltz. Words and images may vanish, but no one ever forgets how to dance. Hannah Higgins felt the weight she'd put on and her eyes grew uneasy. She clung tightly to Elizabeth Morris's hand. Their dancing was deliberate, almost mannered. They held each other at arm's length and moved with a pretty, balanced swing. "We're doing nicely, aren't we?" Elizabeth said. Hannah Higgins nodded and smiled quickly. They had lots of room—there was an empty space all around them.

The moon had gone behind some clouds, and the wind continued to rise. There was rain in the air. The music reached out to the parking lot very faintly, but the ocean was already roaring. Evelyn Peabody sat on an empty box being miserable about all the trouble she'd caused. She wondered if everyone in the Senior Club despised her very much. The wind was damp and she longed for her knit shawl but didn't dare go in to get it. Sometimes life was absolutely awful, and it always seemed to be worst when she had tried to be nice.

"Peabody, have you got a cold?" Thompson asked.

"I'm miserable," she answered curtly. He filled his mouth with air and blew it out very slowly. "Miserable," he said finally. "My friend Jeremiah Spennert was very particularly interested in misery. He used to talk about it often. He talked about people who think misery is the exception and are hurt and surprised when things go bad for them. He knew it was the other way around, just exactly the other way around!" Thompson lay down on the ground and rested his head on his hand. "Don't make sorrow a game," he added a few moments later. "That's what Jeremiah Spennert always used to say."

"Don't lie on the ground," Peabody burst out angrily. "You could get pneumonia!" Now she wanted to go home to bed. She wanted her shawl. They could think what they liked in there.

The Cotillion swayed on through its second round, and like a solitary buoy in the sea, Miss Frey stood and watched the whole city dance by. Tim Tellerton came dancing down the room in laborious small circles; his lady moved quite independently of the music and talked without a break and never took her eyes from his. Tellerton's smile concealed a great desperation. Catherine Frey recognized desperation no matter where she met it, she who lived so close to helplessness. It serves him right, she thought, a liar, spoiled rotten through and through! They danced by very close to her, and all at once without thinking Frey called out "Telephone! Telephone for Mr. Tellerton!" In the door to the lobby she explained briefly that there was no phone call. "My name is Frey. I do the books at the Berkeley Arms. I got the feeling you didn't want to dance."

"That was very nice of you," replied Tim Tellerton seriously. She shrugged her shoulders and they stood next to each other for a moment and watched the dance. The Cotillion went into its third round.

"Excuse me," said Peabody, slipping quickly, mouselike, into the ballroom. And just then the music was cut off by a shriek. A woman screamed several times and then there was total silence. In the middle of the floor lay a little fat man with his head down and his legs drawn up. "It's the Mayor," someone whispered nearby. "He never did like to dance . . . " The orchestra struck up a slow fox-trot. The nurse in street clothes came bounding in from the cloak room and the Mayor was carried away. No one could see his face. Tim Tellerton put his hand in his pocket and closed it around the flower he had been given. It was an hibiscus, withered. They wither almost instantly.

"Let me introduce you," said Mrs. Rubinstein, her eyes coal black. "Tim Tellerton, Miss Peabody." She took Peabody by the arm, a gentle but firm grip that conveyed a command, an order to keep herself under control. "The roses, Miss Peabody," he said automatically. "The rose has always been my favorite flower. Shall we dance?" Evelyn Peabody was seized by confusion, the confusion that always came over her when a lot of things happened all at once and she knew she had to do what was expected of her. She couldn't think of anything to say and she couldn't get into time with the music. No one was dancing under the chandelier, which was where the Mayor had fallen. It was wrong to be dancing right now, it was heartless. She didn't feel well, her head was spinning. "I don't know," she said finally. "I really don't know . . . He always wanted to go home by nine o'clock."

"Did you know him?" Tellerton asked.

"No. But to die right in the middle of the Spring Ball!" The people around her seemed to have lost their senses. First they would glide away like lightning, away and down, and then come rushing toward her again from the other side. The whole room was crooked. She tried to look up at Tellerton, hastily, and saw nothing but a lot of white teeth, way too many. Maybe he had periodontitis. That made them stick out that way. But of course not Tim Tellerton, that couldn't happen to him . . . Her shawl was still in the alcove. Peabody came to a sudden stop and mumbled something about the night breeze. She made a little bob that looked like a curtsy, grabbed up her shawl, and fled from the Senior Club.

Thompson was rolled up behind a car—but he wasn't asleep. She kept telling him they had to go home. "You're right, Peabody, you're absolutely right," he said. "We've got to go home." He climbed to his feet and found his cane and they left the parking lot, crossed the pier, and walked out into the great grassy darkness. Her dress slapped like a sail in the wind. She was feeling better now, and warmer. In the old days, petticoats were always made of taffeta and rustled when you walked. She took off her glasses and cried. It was nice walking through the grass. There were hundreds of white yachts bobbing in the waves along the shore, but none of them were showing lights. She turned and shouted into the wind: "The Mayor died in the middle of the Cotillion!"

"What?" said Thompson.

"The Mayor from Ohio! He died in the middle of the Cotillion! He looked awful lying there on the floor."

"Peabody," said Thompson, "listen to me. They all look awful when they're lying on the floor. My friend Jeremiah Spennert used to say, 'So what? It's not worth brooding about. They're finished—and maybe they've learned something.' "

Peabody just went on crying, from tension and exhaustion, for all the people who died from dancing and for all the people who never got to dance. She dried her eyes with her shawl. She was having a hard time finding her way through the dark. It began to rain.

"Peabody," said Thompson sternly, "now that's enough. Did you really care about the Mayor?"

"No! Not about him, not about anybody! But people's lives are so sad!"

"What did you say? What was that last thing you said?"

"I said people's lives are so sad," Peabody shouted. "You can't help feeling sorry for them."

"Bullshit," said Thompson. "Peabody, there's something wrong with you. If you'll stop and think about it you'll discover you don't feel sorry for anyone in the whole world, but you don't dare stop and think." He stepped off into a flower bed and threw up, and then he said he thought Second Avenue was farther to the east. They were coming up toward the city. The rain got harder and the streetlights swayed slowly back and forth above the black windows in the houses and the bright green trees and bushes sighing in the wind. "One time Papa took us out to a river and the weather was just like this and we took shelter in an empty house. It was a wonderful old house with holes in the floors. I lay down and went to sleep, and there was a branch with green leaves growing straight in through the window, right over my head."

"Peabody, I can't hear what you're saying," Thompson said. "I won't be able to hear another word of what anyone says to me tonight."

They came back to the Berkeley Arms and left each other in the vestibule. The rain went on all night, an almost tropical rain that was very beneficial for the long coastline bordering the Gulf of Mexico.

13 The next morning the rain had let up and was falling as softly as a whisper. The whole house slept. As the morning wore on they came out onto the veranda one by one, but there was no conversation. At one o'clock, Mrs. Rubinstein went to the corner room and presented her green ribbon to Miss Ruthermer-Berkeley. The ribbon was pinned up on the wall beside other green ribbons.

"It is a riddle to me," said the owner of the Berkeley Arms. "It is really astonishing the way you always manage to come up with a hat that is prettier than all the others." Mrs. Rubinstein smiled. "It's not the hat," she said. "It's the way I wear the hat. And I can assure you, Miss Ruthermer-Berkeley, that the same thing is true of my will power. It is possible, on occasion, that I am wrong, but I almost always manage to convey the impression that I am right. Only pure fear can stand in the way of the things I set out to accomplish."

"I believe you," the old woman said. "I am convinced that what you tell me is quite true." She played with her watch chain in silence for a moment. "I understand from Miss Frey," she said finally, "that two of our ladies danced with each other at the ball last night. Some of the more conservative members are said to have been very upset. Mrs. Rubinstein, do you think you could make use of your persuasive talents to give the ladies in question a discreet warning? Of course their behavior was quite harmless, but if their example were followed by others, it could lead to aggravation."

"Aggravation?" said Mrs. Rubinstein. "Why should it lead to anything except that the poor things would finally get to dance? And the poor gentlemen would no longer have to?"

Miss Ruthermer-Berkeley admitted that that seemed right and reasonable, but what was right was not always what was wise. "Personally," she said, "I am quite broadminded, but in a city like St. Petersburg, customs have to be observed. Our traditions are very old. And Miss Frey is not always the best person to convey messages of a personal nature." She did not like this conversation and began slowly massaging her hands. She glanced up with a small, concluding nod.

By two o'clock, the rain was hardly more than a light mist. The three ladies took a stroll in the back yard.

"But why?" said Hannah Higgins. "We danced very well, and didn't step on anyone's toes. Why should anyone mind?"

"Forget about it," said Elizabeth Morris. "People are so peculiar, and getting older doesn't make them any better." Johanson walked by with a container full of something important.

"Most people," said Mrs. Rubinstein, "most people simply mess around. They absolutely dabble. They live out of habit. They fuss with a lot of small things to distract their minds. You, Elizabeth," she went on, turning suddenly to Mrs. Morris, "what do you do with your time? Have you achieved that state of perfect being that requires no evasions? Have you the courage to do nothing at all?"

"Well, that does sound a little extreme," said Elizabeth Morris lightly. She adjusted her hair and went off to sit on the veranda.

"Rebecca, dear," said Mrs. Higgins, "now you've scared her away again. I think she needs to be left in peace. Sometimes a person doesn't really know what she wants and what it's all supposed to mean."

Mrs. Rubinstein gave a long, hoarse laugh. "Is it possible?" she said. "Have you really discovered that these ladies don't know what they want after such long lives? And that they don't have the slightest idea what it's all supposed to mean?"

Hannah Higgins thought it over for a moment and replied earnestly that that was pretty much what she did think.

Johanson came back without the container but carrying an unidentifiable tool in one hand, and disappeared among the bushes, several more of which had come into bloom during the night.

At about three o'clock, it started to rain again. Tim Tellerton came across the street to pay his respects. Peabody saw him coming and leaped to her feet searching for something to say, anything at all, explanations, excuses . . . He stopped at the foot of the steps and asked if they were all well, and Peabody couldn't think of a single pretty little lie to repair the unfortunate evening, to conceal it and stitch it together. "No, I'm afraid not," she burst out. "Two of our rocking chairs are empty . . . But come in and sit down, don't stand there in the rain. And isn't it nice that we're getting some rain?"

"To make things grow," said Mrs. Rubinstein, rocking angrily. "New sprouts, new birds and bees, everything starting all over again. New senior citizens. Have a seat!" Peabody got on her nerves. Peabody in a tailspin was enough to unnerve anyone. Tellerton looked from the rocking chairs to Mrs. Rubinstein. He did not sit down. "Don't mind me," she said. "Sometimes I just throw words around."

"Everything starting all over again from the beginning!" shouted Thompson triumphantly. "Everything over and over again, the same way women talk! Have you ever seen one mending a run in a stocking? Have you ever seen that? They'll do anything to fix a run. Jeremiah Spennert would have thrown the damned stockings in the bay!"

Tim Tellerton stood there and gazed at them. Finally he asked if Miss Frey was anywhere about, but she was not.

"You'll have to forgive us," said Hannah Higgins. "Perhaps we'll see you another time. Some days are simply too eventful, and we're not used to events. I think everyone needs a little time to think."

"That's true," said Tellerton. He bowed respectfully to Lady Higgins and left the veranda.

Sunday came, and Tim Tellerton went down to the harbor. There wasn't much else to do. There was the harbor for those with strong legs and the City Park for those without. The pier was crowded and looked like any cheerful seaside resort. There were small white boats headed out to sea in the sunshine, and the people were all wearing summer colors. Many of them had brought their children, and the parking lot was full of cars. Two busses stood waiting outside the *Bounty* palisade. A ukulele kept repeating the same soft comfort and the children shrieked like birds, running around everywhere until their parents called them back with birdlike whistles. A big friendly family Sunday. Tellerton paid his money at the ticket booth along with everyone else and walked into the subtropical garden. Joe stood by the gangway helping the tourists on board. "Hi," he said. "Aloha!" He gave every lady a plastic hibiscus. He had a lot of people this morning and there was a long line. Halfway along was a stout older gentleman with very pretty eyes who was nervously trying to get his attention. "Hi," Joe said. "Aloha. Is everything all right?" When Tim Tellerton smiled, Joe recognized him. "Oh, hi," he said again. "Nice Sunday weather today!"

And the lovely day passed on toward evening, and the white boats came cruising back into the harbor. The lamps in the ship's rigging were turned on at the appointed hour. The people disappeared—up into town or off toward Tampa, or Sarasota, or someplace far inland. They got into their cars and drove away. St. Petersburg was again a silent city.

When Tim Tellerton got back to Friendship's Rest he took a bath and lay down to rest. He was troubled by the boy on the *Bounty*. Someone ought to help him, talk to him and try to get him to see that time was not unlimited. It went quickly, more and more quickly, and he would have to be careful with it. He had to find meaningful work. Tim Tellerton knew that nothing could be squandered as easily as beauty. It was seldom esteemed at its full value while it stood in bloom, and later on it was preserved at the expense of far too much trouble and despair. Waste depressed him, waste without meaning and foresight. All his life he had repudiated happenstance, uncertain investments, fireworks, expressions of emotional excess that left a person unprotected by a margin of safety, and, most of all, letting time slip by as if it had no value. His own time had come to a stop.

When he closed his eyes, his Pictures instantly appeared—what he called his Pictures: dark enlargements with sharp details, what he had lost, and never gained, and in rapid succession all his rooms one after the other, hotel rooms and stairwells and closed doors, room after room, all very quiet. He tried to think of the Sunday people wandering along the pier, and he himself in their midst, a carefree, friendly day in lovely weather. They didn't know who I was—only one of them knew. I would like to help him, but everything's become so hard to explain. He won't accept or reject what I tell him, it will just be something an old man said.

14

Mrs. Thompson arrived at the Berkeley Arms without giving Mr. Thompson any warning whatsoever. One day there she stood on the veranda, asking for her husband in a manner that seemed threatening. She was a little, bony woman, with a wig and sharp, dark brown eyes. She had a way of lowering her head and looking over the tops of her glasses that was disturbing, as if some very small bull were considering an attack.

No one told her that Thompson had gone to Palmer's. Thelma Thompson sat down on the veranda to wait. She took out some knitting and told them in short, choppy sentences about her trip from Iowa. A nasty driver, a dirty hotel across from the bus station, and then she told them how many years it had taken to track down Thompson's address.

"And to think he's been married the whole time,"

said Frey, and Mrs. Thompson looked at her over the tops of her glasses and snorted.

Peabody was getting more and more concerned. Someone had to warn him. It was absolutely essential to prepare the poor man for what had happened. A sudden shock could be dangerous. She stood up suddenly and declared that she was hungry, and Mrs. Thompson immediately put away her knitting and said that she was too. They walked in silence to the Garden. It was packed, and the food line started at the door, old people moving forward one step at a time. They pushed their trays along the counter unbelievably slowly and selected this dish or that from among the salad plates and the desserts. Kidney, hamburger, and sausage were the entrees for the day. The fabulously ancient Mrs. Bovary shuffled along directly in front of them. She was having a great deal of trouble making up her mind. Her hands and her head shook violently. Poor Mrs. Bovary, thought Peabody, does she have to take jello every time? And Mrs. Bovary took some jello, because she liked it, and the whole thing shook out over the edge of the plate and down into the kidneys. She tried to fish it out, but had no luck.

"Here, I'll do that," said Mrs. Thompson and stretched out one long arm, but the old woman didn't want her help. "Mind your own business," she hissed, and went on without any jello.

"Oh, excuse me," Peabody mumbled, and took some kidneys although she hated kidneys. She was very muddled. They were near the cashier now, and she waited for the usual scene over Mrs. Bovary's tray. The waiter tried to grab it, but the old woman held on with both hands. "You blasted nigger, I'll carry it myself," she said. "Can't you ever learn?" And the black man grinned and they carried the tray together to the nearest table. It looked strange.

"I see," said Mrs. Thompson. "So you're not allowed to carry your own tray."

"No, you're not. And you have to tip the waiter. So it's a good idea to have the money in your hand, because they're in a hurry, and if you're not quick they just shrug their shoulders and think you're stingy."

"Fiddlesticks," said Mrs. Thompson.

The Garden was a large, attractive room painted to look like a jungle. There were mangrove swamps with masses of roots that twisted in the air, and snakes and monkeys hung from the crowns of the trees, and the palm trees bent at the ceiling and grew out over their heads.

"The artist is said to have been inspired by Silver Springs," said Miss Peabody, making conversation. "We're going there from the Berkeley Arms next week. We're going to take a trip on the jungle river. They've got an aquarium and a snake farm, too. Is this your first time in Florida?"

"My first and my last," Mrs. Thompson replied.

The kidneys tasted terrible. Kidneys were no good with jello. "Excuse me," said Peabody, "I have to go out for a moment . . ."

She felt better when she got out on the street.

Thompson was sitting on his usual stool. "Peabody," he said. "Do you want a beer?"

"Not now," she said. "I've come to warn you. You have a visitor. A woman. She's looking for you. Right now she's over at the Garden having lunch . . ."

"What kind of a woman? What woman?"

"Your wife!" cried Peabody with her eyes aghast. "She's found you!"

Thompson slid from his bar stool and started toward the door in instinctive flight. Then he turned and came back. He was clearly and obviously scared.

Peabody looked toward the bartender. "Please sir, could you give him a little glass of something strong?" she said. Thompson downed it in one gulp and then stood still with his huge eyebrows drawn together tightly. More than ever, he looked like an angry, frightened ape. Peabody put her hand on his arm and gave it a sympathetic squeeze, and then she hurried back to the Garden.

Thompson didn't come back to the Berkeley Arms. Later that afternoon Miss Frey called Palmer's, but he had left there long ago. Thelma Thompson stood beside the telephone staring accusingly over the tops of her glasses. "What now?" she said. "What are you going to do now? Can't you call some other bar?"

"Don't look at me, it's not my fault," said Frey angrily. "And if I were going to call anyplace, it would be the hospital."

"An accident?" Mrs. Thompson burst out. "But why? He's been all right for eighteen years. For eighteen years I've been waiting for this day, and then he disappears the minute I arrive! He can't have gone and died somewhere before I got a chance to talk to him, he can't have done it on purpose!"

"Did he know?" asked Mrs. Rubinstein and looked at Peabody, a long hard look.

"No, what do you mean?" Peabody said. "Oh, it's dreadful." She heard Frey calling the hospitals, one after the other, and finally she went to her room and lay down on the bed with the quilt over her head. Her conscience painted a long series of tragic pictures of everything that could have happened. Maybe he'd drunk too much beer and broken his neck. Maybe he'd fled on the first bus out of town and was wandering around in some strange desolate place without any money, far from all human help. He might even have thrown himself in the bay! She hadn't warned him gently enough. She should have remembered that it was always better to leave decisions to other people and not let yourself be misled by compassion. Once again, Peabody had made herself miserable, and there was no one to talk her out of it.

At five o'clock, Frey called the police.

Meanwhile, Mr. Thompson was asleep under some bushes in the City Park. The bushes had reminded him of a thicket behind his mother's house, a perfectly wonderful thicket where he used to hide from his mother and his aunts. The ground was warm and dry. Sometimes he would wake up for a little while, wake up and then go back to sleep again. He hadn't slept so well for a long time.

Late that evening, Thompson crawled out of the bushes. It was very hard to get to his feet and almost impossible to straighten his back. Carefully, a few steps at a time, he limped back to the Berkeley Arms. All the lights were out. Very deliberately, he went through all his bureau drawers and suitcases and searched out all the papers that bore his name, papers that attested or confirmed or certified, or that legally, statistically, professionally, religiously, or simply socially incorporated Alexander Thompson into the society in which he lived. He put all of it into the fireplace in the vestibule. For good measure, he sat down on the floor in the big dark room and tore apart and crumpled up a number of women's magazines, and then he lit the fire. Thompson did not know that the fireplace was a mere decoration without a flue, in fact an exact copy of an English fireplace that Miss Ruthermer-Berkeley's parents had admired. The vestibule and the staircase filled instantly with smoke. He opened the veranda door, but the smoke continued up the stairs in a billowing wave. It was as if his whole sinful life were crying to heaven in smoke and flames.

"Linda!" he screamed. He banged on her door and bellowed. "Linda! Now I've done it!"

Linda and Joe came running out, naked in the red glow from the fire.

"There isn't any flue!" Thompson explained. "I didn't know! I didn't know there wasn't any flue!" His eyes were running and he started to cough.

"It's just paper," Joe said. "It'll burn out in a minute."

"What's he saying? What'd he say?" Thompson said.

"It will go out in a minute. Everything will be all right. Please, Joe, go back to bed. They will be scared if they see you without any clothes. I'll open a window upstairs." She pulled a dress over her head and hurried up the stairs. The hall was full of pungent smoke. She opened the door to the corner room a crack and called softly, "Mrs. Morris? May I open your window? There is something wrong with the flue and the smoke won't go out."

A light was burning over the bed.

"Is it a big fire?" asked Elizabeth Morris with the sheet up over her nose. She wasn't wearing her teeth.

"No, very small. I thought it would be best to air it out here in your room."

"Why my room?"

Linda smiled. "Because you're so calm," she said. "I'll come back and close the window when the fire has gone out."

"Fire!" screamed Miss Frey out on the stairs. She clutched the railing and stumbled down into the smoke-filled vestibule. Charred papers sailed around her like bats—and there stood Thompson! Thompson, with the fire tongs in his hand, his face crooked and his hair on end. In the glare from the fire he looked more infernal than ever. "Dreadful man!" cried Frey in anguish. "Where have you been? Are you trying to burn us all alive? Here we've been calling the hospitals and the police and all the time you're still alive! What are you doing? What are you trying to do?"

Thompson stared at her feet and explained that

there wasn't any flue. This fireplace didn't have a flue. And he was especially deaf today and couldn't hear what she was saying.

"But at least he's alive," Peabody whispered. "He's alive. It's not my fault . . . "

No one had thought to put on the overhead light, and the blazing fire turned the vestibule into a ghastly, alien place. The pillars threw fluttering shadows on the walls.

"Deaf," said Miss Frey to herself. "You make yourselves deaf and you make yourselves dumb. You don't know how lucky you are." She opened the door to the back yard, and the smoke blew out into the night on the gentle cross-draft.

At eight o'clock the next morning, Mrs. Thompson returned to the Berkeley Arms. Only Linda was up. She was vacuuming the vestibule.

"Did he come back?" asked Thompson's wife.

"Yes," Linda said. Thelma Thompson sat down on the veranda and took out her knitting. She looked tired. Her face had become a small closed square below her wig. She was quiet today. The residents at the Berkeley Arms went to their breakfast and came back again and still she didn't speak. They sat beside each other in their rocking chairs and looked at the street and at Friendship's opposite.

Mr. Thompson appeared at eleven o'clock, in his black suit. He had put on his hearing aid. Without any hesitation, he limped up to his wife and said, "Thelma.

What a surprise to see you in St. Petersburg. I hope you're in good health." His voice was completely altered, a voice they had never heard before.

"My health!" said Thelma Thompson with violent intensity. "You haven't shown any interest in my health for the last eighteen years."

"What did you say?" Thompson asked. "I didn't hear you."

"For eighteen years you never cared how I was!"

He shook his head and turned his great, hairy ear toward her mouth, and she began to shout. "You deserted me!" She forgot everything but her rage. "You ran away," she screamed, "you ran away and left me with the dogs and the garden and the whole anniversary party with thirty guests!"

"What is my wife saying?" asked Thompson anxiously. "Has something terrible happened?"

Mrs. Rubinstein observed that the TV room was at their disposal in the event the Thompsons had personal matters to discuss.

"Discuss!" howled Thelma Thompson. "You can't discuss anything with him!"

"Maybe I can help," said Mrs. Morris. "Let's write down what you want to say, it's a very good way to do it. What shall I write?"

Mrs. Thompson glared angrily at the tablet on Mrs. Morris's lap. "Incredible," she said. "Write: You left me without a word. Why?"

Thompson raised his glasses and read. "I was tired," he said. "I wrote you a letter and told you I was tired."

"What next?" said Mrs. Morris.

"This doesn't work," said Mrs. Thompson. "It isn't a real conversation!"

Mrs. Higgins leaned forward. "Did you like him?" she asked. "Back then, eighteen years ago?"

"No. No, I didn't."

"Do you like him now?"

Thelma Thompson laughed. "Don't make me laugh," she said.

"But what is it you want?"

And what was it she wanted? What was she after? She wanted to speak her piece at last and be done with it, she wanted to see what was left of him after eighteen years, to find out if he was ashamed, if he was sorry, to find out what she had done, why he had left her the whole house, whether he had found something important that she knew nothing about. How could she talk about what she wanted? How could she know? It had been hard to find him, nearly impossible, and it had been expensive, and eventually she couldn't think about anything but finding him and talking, talking for hours, for days, and then finally everything would be said, finished, over and done with, peaceful at last.

"What shall I write?" said Elizabeth Morris.

Thelma Thompson stood up. "Write that no one can talk to a person who never answers," she shouted. "Write that there are people who can't stand things to smell bad and always be a mess! Write that little, kindly friends are better than evil, intelligent ones! Write anything you want, write for a year and you won't have written half of it!" She rushed across the veranda with her knitting in her hand, away, to the hotel, to the bus, to Iowa. Her face was blotched with red and she was crying.

"Thelma," said Thompson, and grabbed her by the coat. "Thelma Thompson. You're going now, and we won't see each other again, and I haven't heard a word you said. I'm sorry. I'm very sorry. Believe me, I was impossible from start to finish."

Mrs. Thompson stood there for a moment without looking at him. Then she walked firmly out to the street. They could hear her footsteps for quite a long time. No one said anything. Mrs. Morris drew big circles on her tablet, one empty circle after another in a long row.

After Thelma Thompson's visit, Thompson's rocking chair was always empty. He read in his room, screened off from the limited world of the others. Day by day, book by book, he realized more and more clearly that she had taken the sting out of his commentaries and spoiled the pleasure they gave him. These books in their immense simplicity were no longer worthy of his irony. Memories he had long since disposed of came back to torture him, and his sleep at night was harried by frightening dreams. He dreamed that the house burned down. He had burned down the whole house, and the reproachful, charred bodies of women were dragged from the ashes. Plaintive ladies prowled around in the bushes outside his window and pressed their faces against the glass. They ran after him on the street; he could hear their heels behind him. They were everywhere. And the house burned every night.

He poured water in the can for his cigarette butts, but it didn't help. On his way to Palmer's, or sitting peacefully beside his glass of beer, the poor man would be seized with doubt and rush home to make sure there was no fire in his room. Several times he passed Johanson in the garden without looking up from the ground. One day Johanson stopped him and asked him how he was, if there wasn't anything he'd like to borrow. But Thompson just shook himself and walked on by.

For the most part he sat by his window, which was shaded by the huge green leaves on the trees. Early summer had burst forth in its full luxuriance, shadowing and sheltering his room. Thompson invented a new game. His world was a jungle. The jungle outside his window grew denser and denser and he let a frenzied vegetation cover all St. Petersburg. Vines crept stealthily onto every veranda, muffling every sound and bringing the rocking chairs to a halt. Lush jungle filled the city. Inside the abandoned houses and along the overgrown streets crept wild animals, untamed and unpredictable, tigresses and female chimpanzees, impossible to fence out and impossible to understand. This vision of the world as a jungle was a comfort to Thompson, and gradually the house stopped burning. Sometimes on the stairs, in a doorway, he would hurl an accusation. "Peabody," he'd say, "are you living an honest life?" Or he would frighten Miss Frey. "Hey, you old flirt! Do you know what you're living for?" And to Mrs. Rubinstein he said, "You are a monument. You died a long time ago, and now you're a monument." She stood there with a cigarette in one hand, and her black eyes gazed at him from under cream-colored lids. "I'm glad you're over the worst of it," she said. "As a matter of fact, I have felt monumental for the last thirty years." Thompson cackled and walked on through his jungle.

15 Hannah Higgins was crocheting lacework borders on a pillowcase. "Elizabeth, dear," she said, "I've been thinking a lot about Thelma Thompson's visit. There are so few families that are happy together. I thank God every day that I'm so close to mine."

"But you hardly ever see them," Elizabeth Morris said.

"You can be close to people without actually seeing them," Mrs. Higgins explained. "Surely you know that —you're so wise." They were sitting on a bench in the City Park, quite early in the day. The morning was the best time. There were too many people later on.

"They've sent me a song," said Hannah Higgins. "My brother's boy, the trumpet player, sent me a lullaby." She opened her purse and showed the letter. "Look how nicely he writes music. Just like little birds on branches."

Elizabeth Morris read the music and said it was good, personal.

Mrs. Higgins flushed. "Lord above," she said. "How wonderful! How lovely! You sit there and read music the way anyone else would read the paper. Can you play too?"

"I'll play it for you this evening."

Mrs. Higgins leaned back on the park bench and clasped her hands on her ample stomach and laughed, from deep inside a sense of personal harmony with the way things always turned out for the best.

"It's too hot here in the sun," said Mrs. Morris, getting up. She felt a sudden, senseless irritation.

The piano was very old. It was white, like everything else in the vestibule, and covered with a silk cloth.

"It's not really in tune," said Elizabeth Morris.

"I suppose not," Mrs. Higgins nodded, "but it doesn't matter."

"It doesn't matter?" said Mrs. Morris shrilly. "It doesn't matter that the piano's out of tune?"

Hannah Higgins looked at the floor and said she was sorry. She was always saying stupid things, never seemed to realize what was important to other people.

"Sit down and listen," Elizabeth Morris said. "First I'll play just the melody, very simply."

It was a honky-tonk piano from the turn of the century. The notes burst forth in thin splinters, and inside the old neglected instrument the strings whirred like in a music box. She listened, fascinated by this long-forgotten form of music, this different means of expression.

"Now listen carefully," she said. "Here it is in classical form. And then I'll play it as a waltz."

Hannah Higgins listened.

Finally, Elizabeth Morris played the melody as saloon music, as honky-tonk, and the piano woke up and gave her more than she had expected. Ostensibly stumbling, brittle to the breaking point, arrogantly rhythmical, the lullaby rocked through the Berkeley Arms, as clear as water in its simplicity. Suddenly she stopped and swung around on her stool. "Which did you like best?" she said.

"The first and the last," Hannah Higgins whispered. "My, that must make you happy."

Miss Frey and Peabody stood on the stairs applauding. Mrs. Rubinstein didn't move. She was the only one who realized what an unusually fine pianist Elizabeth Morris was.

"Honky-tonk!" Peabody cried. "Oh please!"

And Mrs. Morris continued to play, alone with her famous and celebrated sense for the faltering rhythm and the brilliant false note.

Three old ladies came over from Friendship's to listen. No one knew their names.

Miss Ruthermer-Berkeley pressed the button at the head of her bed. "Linda, my child," she said. "Open the door so I can hear the music. Are the ladies dancing?"

"Yes," Linda said.

"Then would you mind moving the furniture so they'll have more room?"

Mrs. Morris played all evening. A number of people stood listening out on the sidewalk. The music rolled over them with the freshness of spring greenery and with the mournful purity and joy that was born in New Orleans jazz. They danced. When Elizabeth Morris felt that they were tired, she began to play her own film music, a vague, calm background that merely held off the silence. She gave them time. Then she went on to "Alma Mater," which they all knew, a school song, safe and traditional. They came up behind her and gathered around the piano, in the chapel, just before summer vacation. They began to sing in harmony.

Perfect organization, thought Mrs. Rubinstein.

They sang all the verses.

She let the kindled excitement sink to rest, as in love, not abandoning ecstasy to itself but leading it quietly to its conclusion. When the song was over, Mrs. Morris closed the piano and spread the silk cloth over it again. The three ladies from Friendship's thanked them all and went back to their own house.

The next day, Peabody met her on the stairs and burst out, "Oh, Mrs. Morris, I'm so glad you've finally found a hobby."

"A hobby?"

"Yes. Playing the piano. I've been so worried about you. A person really needs something to keep her busy . . . And if you can make yourself useful at the same time, why so much the better!" The mouse smiled shyly, showing many small mouse teeth.

Elizabeth Morris studied Peabody through her dark glasses. "Miss Peabody," she said, "your thoughtfulness is incredible." And she went up to her room. There were fresh flowers on the night table. "They're from our own garden today," Linda said. "They're in all the rooms. They came out last night." The Berkeley Arms maintained a traditional attitude toward flowers. Plastic bouquets were used only in the vestibule.

"Mrs. Morris," Linda said. "May I talk to you about Joe?"

"Of course," said Mrs. Morris. And Linda explained that Joe was not happy. The Jesus people didn't write to him, although they had promised. Jesus might come at any moment, and it was important for Joe to be with them when He did. He couldn't wait by himself. He had to go live like the first Christians and share everything except his motorcycle and find joy before Jesus came. There was no time to lose.

"But my dear child," said Mrs. Morris, taking off her sunglasses and sitting down on the bed, "why don't they write to him? Aren't they his friends?"

"No. He only talked to them on the street in Miami. They promised to write. He saw them dancing. They have all quit their jobs, because Jesus could come any day."

Mrs. Morris thought Joe should go find them, but he couldn't do that. The letter was a sign, and he had to wait until it came. "What a nuisance," she said. "No wonder it worries you." She paused for a moment and said, "Do you think these people are good for Joe?"

"I don't know."

"What if they disappoint him?"

"They must not disappoint him," Linda said. "He couldn't take it."

"And what about you?"

"I have put everything in the Madonna's hands."

Elizabeth Morris sighed. "In that case," she said, "what I have to say doesn't make much difference." When Linda opened the door to go, she said, "Don't worry, Linda. Most things tend to work out if we're only patient."

"That was what I wanted to hear," said Linda with a smile. "The Madonna will arrange everything for the best, but the waiting is so lonely."

16 Tim Tellerton went to Macy's and bought a gift book with shiny illustrations. The book was called *With These Two Hands,* and told about all the great men who had started out with nothing. With Best Wishes from Tim Tellerton.

It was Monday and the *Bounty* was closed. "Try at the swimming stadium," they told him at the gas station. He strolled south along the shore, across sandy fields and over the long green slopes of the golf course. He was in no hurry. The freshness of the morning and the endless, empty beach gave him a feeling of anticipation. There were no waves on the bay today, but there was a steady roar from the surf. On the land side, a row of white houses lay sleeping in the distance. He arrived at the pool. Surrounded by marble terraces and long arcades, it lay open to the sky near the water. Sometimes a day had a kind of purity, and all of its colors were astonishingly clear. This was one of them. Outside, beside Joe's Honda, stood a row of bright bicycles shining in the sun, looking like multicolored insects ready for flight. The swimming pool was as pretty as all swimming pools—green, transparent, rippling with small pointed waves and full of screaming children. At the shallow end, some senior citizens were swimming gravely back and forth along the edge. Bounty Joe was diving. Over and over again he would climb up to the middle board, stand for a long time, waiting, collecting himself in anxious concentration, and then dive, over and over again. Tellerton bought a newspaper at the stand and sat down in the shade under one of the arcades. All the tables were empty. With a rare feeling of peace, he listened to the children playing—again these thin birdlike cries of delight and the sound of splashing water, a world of coolness and distance, part of the morning itself.

Joe came over to his table. "Hi," he said. "Aloha. I'm practicing for the high board."

"How come?" asked Tellerton. "Are you going to compete?"

"No, I just like to dive."

The book lay on the marble table top. "It's for you," said Tellerton. "I saw it in the window as I was walking by the store and I thought you might like it."

"But why should you give me a present?"

"Sometimes," said Tellerton, "sometimes there isn't any reason for what you do—you just act on impulse."

"Sure, of course," Joe said. He was embarrassed. "It was nice of you. Aren't you coming out in the sun?"

"I don't know if you care about autographs," Tim Tellerton said. "But I brought along some of the usual kind for your friends." The signature was small, finely written on heavy cream paper. He had a whole bundle of them.

"My hands are all wet," said Bounty Joe.

"Do you like working on the *Bounty*?"

"Yes, it's easy work and a good job."

"Are you interested in ships?"

"Sure. Ships are pretty."

"How did you happen to know who I was?"

"Oh, I just knew," Bounty Joe mumbled, wrapping his arms around his body in growing discomfort. He took a step backward toward the pool.

Tim Tellerton stood up with weary irritation. He folded his paper and realized that he no longer had the necessary patience, the strength that had to be collected and formulated in order to produce a fruitful conversation with a pup, with a young dolphin. He turned to go. What was a conversation, and what could it mean? Mutual consideration of important things. Communication of experience and memory. Construction of possibilities for the future. To clarify and recognize together, and to observe the changes in a glance, a tone of voice, a silence—the silence of hesitation or understanding. To shape without altering. To laugh, or to sit quietly in common shyness that was never expressed.

Joe went with him to the exit. "It looks like a good book. All those men who made good in the old days."

"What do you mean, the old days?" said Tellerton, looking right at Joe. His eyes were like blue jewels.

"The old days! The youngest of them isn't ten years older than you are."

"Ten years," said Joe and smiled. Ten years, that was an endless time, an epoch, an abyss. Everything had happened in the last ten years.

"Haven't you ever wanted to be a shipbuilder or a captain or sail around the world?"

Joe shook his head, very amiably but with concern.

"You can't wear plastic flowers in your hair all your life!"

Joe answered patiently that the old people liked him that way. They liked to pretend they were in Tahiti.

"Aloha!" Tim Tellerton burst out. He spit out the gentle word with contempt and turned on his heel to leave.

Now he's upset, Joe thought. I didn't say what he expected me to say. Old people can be difficult sometimes. It was part of his job to be nice to them, and as a rule he liked them—they were usually satisfied with very little. The only trouble with Tellerton was that he wasn't old enough. He still made a fuss about things he didn't understand. If they only knew! If they only realized that time had run out and their whole ruined world didn't matter any more. It was no longer a question of becoming, of doing, of having! All of a sudden he was furious at the Jesus people, who hadn't written. The letter was his starting signal. Then he would know! Then he could shout to all of them that time had run out! He was coming! Jesus! He would wear that radiant name on his bike, on his clothes, in orange and green and purple as he dove into the ocean in Miami. He was wearing it already, except that he'd turned his bathing suit inside out. As if in the rigging of a ship, Joe climbed up to the highest board and roared, "Aloha!" and dived. It was a very poor dive and he almost broke his back.

17 Sometimes in the evenings Elizabeth Morris would play and the ladies from Friendship's Rest would come over to dance with each other. Tellerton did not come back, but it did happen that solitary wanderers would come up onto the veranda to listen, or stop for a while at the gate before continuing on their way.

One evening a tall thin man came into the vestibule and said that his name was McKenzie and that he came from Scotland, Europe. The music had drawn him in—it was so happy. "Go right on playing," he said. "Don't mind me!" McKenzie didn't want to sit down. Standing in the middle of the room, he told them he was in town for just one night, one single night, and then he was going on to Yucatan, which he had wanted to visit all his life. They all sat down in the wicker chairs and looked at him. Mrs. Morris went on playing, but very softly, almost inaudibly. "Ladies, I'm an old man, and if

I don't travel now I never will." McKenzie was somehow alarming. His every movement was carried out with a kind of failing sluggishness, as if his tall thin body might at any moment fold up and disintegrate, and his smile had the same fragility. It conveyed a lifetime of patient, apologetic smiles. "Yes, Yucatan is a very inaccessible country, and the language is a problem. But they love music. They have a warm temperament."

"Mr. McKenzie," said Mrs. Rubinstein from her chair, "I suppose you are on a tour."

"Oh, no!" he answered eagerly. "I'm traveling alone."

"Into Yucatan?"

"A short way, just far enough to take me through some real jungle. I've read everything about Yucatan."

"It is very hot," said Mrs. Rubinstein. "And the people are very savage, and there aren't any busses through the jungle."

"I know," said McKenzie almost bashfully. "It's a dreadful place. But if I don't go now I never will." Miss Frey asked if he wouldn't like to sit down and have a Coca-Cola, but he didn't think so, he was only passing by.

"What a shame you can't stay longer in St. Petersburg," said Miss Peabody. "It's such a lovely city." It was hard to look him in the face from a sitting position. He was too tall.

"No, no," he said. "I haven't a single day to lose." And he smiled at each one of them in turn.

"How long are you going to stay in Mexico?" Miss Frey asked. But he only smiled. Mrs. Morris, trying to help, began to play a Scottish ballad. McKenzie listened, with a frightened look, and then suddenly started to sing, an octave too high. The voice had the same uncertain frailty as the man himself. The song was very long and the words were pretty—mostly about heaths and fogs and sails that never returned. Every time he approached the chorus, the ladies held their breath and looked at the floor. After the final chorus, the entire vestibule applauded.

"Scotland!" cried Miss Peabody. "The moors! It must be wonderful!"

"It's fine," McKenzie said.

He's about to cry, thought Mrs. Morris angrily, and she started in on another ballad. He began singing immediately. They're all the same, singing away their distance from some geographical place, a dot on the map that they can't ever leave behind. So much feeling and so little talent. The words don't vary much: a thousand miles from home, a train wailing in the distance, the green green grass where they were born, the endless hills of home. She helped him over the worst parts with little runs, but she played like a whisper where his voice held. Today it's Scottish. Tomorrow some German in tears. Or someone from Illinois, or the Carolinas, anyone who isn't from St. Petersburg.

At one time, her listeners had only listened, anonymous in their darkness, their faces white smears, their applause rolling toward her like the surf. They had gradually drawn closer until now she had them right behind her back. And they seldom noticed the music until she had stopped playing.

McKenzie got another round of applause. Elizabeth Morris let her hands sink into her lap, and suddenly, unexpectedly and unforgivably, she was seized by a crushing homesickness.

And then he left. In a swarm of good wishes, he took his leave, and they never heard of him again.

18 Early in the mornings, Tim Tellerton would walk across the grassy fields to the swimming stadium and the cool arcades. Sometimes he read his paper, but mostly he just sat there quietly and listened to the shouts of the children and the constant movement of the water in the pool. Occasionally when Bounty Joe came in, he would get up to go, raise his hand in an absent-minded greeting, and return to the city the same way he had come. One morning Joe came over to his table and told him that now he could do the high board.

"I'm glad to hear it," Tellerton said.

Joe ran over to the scaffold and clambered up. "Out of the way!" he yelled at the children down in the pool. The tension hunched his shoulders and he waited too long before he dived. The dive was no good at all. As he swam over to the ladder he noticed that the arcade was empty.

The next day Joe went to Tellerton and told him he'd read the book and hadn't liked it.

"Why not? Was it poorly written?"

"I don't know about that. I just didn't like it."

"Wasn't there anyone in it who could dive?"

Joe got mad. "You're making fun of me," he said. "I want to know why you're making fun of me."

"Just to tease you," said Tellerton straightforwardly. "Can't you stand being teased?"

Joe looked at him for a moment and started to laugh. "Good!" he said. "No, none of them could dive. They were all too old and fat! They never had time to learn how, because all they did was work to get famous, and when they weren't famous any more it was too late to go diving." He jogged around Tellerton's table chanting, "I'm making fun of you, I'm making fun of you!" and then he launched himself into the pool and swam over and back like a madman. When he came up the ladder he was still laughing. It was nice to laugh again. Helpless with mirth, he put his arms around his knees and rocked back and forth.

Their friendship began. Unconcerned and respectful, they amused each other with simple games of words. Joe liked their brief meetings. He would stand at Tellerton's table and talk about whatever occurred to him. Their conversations were often like a game where you weren't allowed to let yourself be hurt. Joe tried to be funny, to come up with childishly disarming remarks. Sometimes he would tease, and when he was tired, he would dive—better and better. Every good dive was worth one point. He counted points for both of them.

Talking to Tellerton was like tossing a coin onto a roulette table or into a wishing well—not for what you
could win but just for fun. You never knew with Tellerton. He was an old man, but he showed Joe respect. He
never harped on things, but he could lose his temper for
no reason at all. He was old in the wrong way, and con-
fusing. One time Joe had had a cat that was sixteen years
old, an ancient cat. With a little patience, you could get
it to play, and chase its own tail, but when it got angry
you had to watch out.

It seemed to Tim Tellerton that every meeting reduced his chances of ever helping Joe, but he didn't
dare talk about serious things. He wanted to hold onto
his morning landscape, his strolls across the grass, this
cool world of green water and light, playful words—the
whole carefree atmosphere that made him feel so calm.

One evening as he was walking along the bayfront,
Bounty Joe drove up beside him. "Hi, Aloha," Joe said,
climbing off and leading his motorcycle. "I'm taking her
to Silver Springs next week, in the morning before the
traffic gets heavy. Look at her. New paint job." They
gazed at the big, gleaming machine rolling softly along
in Joe's hands.

"She's a beauty," Tellerton said.

"Honda," Joe said. "Seventy-one."

"You like machines."

"Yes, I like them."

"Do you know about them? Do you know how they
work?"

"I know everything about her," said Joe contemptuously.

"But she isn't the only one. The whole world is full of fascinating machines. You could study them, make new machines of your own . . . "

"So you're back to that," Joe yelled. "Making! Becoming! I don't want to *become*, I want to *be*. You're talking about a world that ended a long time ago and doesn't mean a thing any more. All that stuff about becoming and making and owning!"

"You own a motorcycle," said Tellerton sharply.

Joe stopped. "Look at her," he said. "You can't own a Honda. Can you own 120 miles an hour? Speed, class—those aren't possessions. Can you own a guitar? Can you own music? It's stupid. You people own things a whole different way."

"What people?"

"You people who've hung on too long. Listen to me." Joe lowered his voice and continued patiently. "You know what I mean. You collect things. Admiration, titles, higher pay—things. Wall to wall carpets. Being famous. And it's all a waste of time, a huge waste of time."

Tim Tellerton didn't answer. Joe walked on beside his bike and tried to explain. "That's all over. It's out. Now people share. What you call ambition and position are out. Try to understand what I'm talking about. None of it's true any more. You've made the world a terrible place to live in . . . "

Tellerton interrupted him. "I recognize all that. I've heard all that before." His heart had started pounding and was making him walk very slowly. He tried to control himself. "And when you dive? Aren't you proud of yourself when it's good? Don't you want to be admired?"

"It's not the same thing," Joe burst out. "Diving is diving. Like just being, just living! You just dive in the water. Don't be dumb."

"It's a wading pool!" said Tellerton. "You hide in a wading pool and you claim the world is ruined and you think flowers in your hair are going to look good on you until the day you die!"

That was wrong. He had to get a grip on himself. Right now he had to speak to Joe, concentrate the best of everything he knew and believed and try to get Joe to wake up. Tell him about the breath-taking possibilities and the helplessness you felt when it was all too late, about life the indestructible that was always worth the trouble, about the joy of shaping and achieving and expressing, and the constant springboards for new triumphs, and the grand mistakes, and the huge surprises, about everything that could be reached and embraced before failing strength got the better of belated insight. What a shame that it was evening. He was tired, and very upset. "The world isn't ruined," he said. "It's still out there. Maybe it's harder to live in now, but we still have it . . ."

Joe interrupted again. "How much do _you_ still have?" he said. "Was being famous all that much fun?" He saw Tellerton go pale with rage and it frightened him. All he wanted to do was get out of here, away, drive like hell and leave everything old behind him.

"Get me a taxi," said Tellerton.

"I'm sorry!" Joe said. "I'm sorry—that was a stupid thing to say! I say stupid things all the time now, but it's only because they don't write. I wait and wait and they don't write and there's so little time left!" He jumped on his motorcycle and roared off toward town.

Joe followed the taxi back to the bay front where Tellerton stood waiting. He held the door.

"Who doesn't write?" Tim Tellerton asked.

"It's just a letter. It was supposed to come to Palmer's."

"Who is it who doesn't write to you?" Tellerton repeated.

"The Jesus people!" Joe shouted. "Jesus is coming back, now, any day, and they promised we'd all be together when He comes!"

Tim Tellerton stepped into the car and Joe closed the door. They drove back to Friendship's Rest and Joe stayed right in front of the taxi all the way, giving it a motorcycle escort the way they did for statesmen, leading home a guide who himself had ceased to travel.

Joe stretched out in the bed and said, "He's strange. He goes to such a lot of trouble just for me."

"He loves you," Linda said. "You should listen to what he says and try to understand. Sometimes old people say very wise things." The light was out. After a while he could tell that she was asleep. The Miami breakers came rolling in toward the beach. They had baptized five hundred people that week alone. He walked across the sand and waded out into the water, drenched with foam, filled with music, Jesus Rock, a hundred guitars playing up on shore. "I named His name, I finally did it. Jesus," Joe whispered, over and over again, but the name was only a name, soft as a whisper, alien. He couldn't find the fire by himself. They had talked to him on the street in Miami. What they had said he didn't remember, merely the stream of words, convincing and warm. And he remembered their absolute certainty. They knew. They never doubted. He had followed them down a long staircase into a darkness that seemed to burst with music. Cones of white light were aimed at the guitars and the drums and at the joyful people dancing with their eyes closed and clapping their hands and embracing each other, swaying forward in an unapproachable faith and trust.

Linda woke up. "Are you having a bad dream?" she asked.

"No," he said. "I'm awake."

Miracles—what were they? Springs in the desert? Making the blind see? Making all the yellow apples in the world turn blue? Why was heaven so stingy with its miracles? Not even the smallest one, not even a postcard! He asked Linda how long a miracle usually took. Linda said that sometimes they only took a second, but sometimes they took very long, almost a whole lifetime.

"A lifetime!" Joe said. "Kiss me. A lifetime." And he turned toward the wall.

That same evening, Tellerton went to Palmer's and found a place to stand at the bar. It was crowded with people, the men who worked in the restaurants and the guesthouses and the bus station. There were some letters stuck in a cigar box beside the cash register. Maybe one of them was for Joe.

"A whisky," he said. "You're having a busy evening."

"Can't complain," the bartender said.

"Not many young people in this town."

"No, not many."

"You never see any Jesus people, do you?"

"Ha," said the bartender. "The only ones we got learned about Jesus in their catechism." And he went on with his work at the other end of the bar.

"You're new here," said the man on his left. He had a large face and tired eyes. "The Jesus people. There aren't any in this town. There isn't anything in this town."

"What do you know about them? How do they live?"

"Live? Why, they live any way they can. They've got something to believe in and they go on living. What else would they do? I'm drunk, but I can tell you one thing, and that's that there's one giant difference, and that's something to believe in. Giant, believe me. Have you got a single person to believe in? Someone you can absolutely count on, I mean, every second?"

"Take it easy," the bartender said as he passed. "This gentleman's from up north. Take it easy."

"Excuse me," said Tellerton's neighbor solemnly. "I must ask you to excuse me. Is there a single person you can absolutely count on?"

"No," said Tellerton politely.

"Herbert," said the bartender. "Easy." He looked at Tellerton. "Another drink?"

"No thank you," Tellerton said. He didn't like alcohol.

Herbert tried to look him in the eye and then looked at the mirror behind the bar and then looked away. After a while he looked at Tellerton again. "Waking up in the morning," he said.

"Yes," said Tellerton.

"Everything's always the same, the past and the future and right now, exactly the same. Call me Herbert. Do you know why waking up in the morning is so awful? Wait a second, I'll explain it to you. It's because there isn't a thing in the world you believe in, not one single thing. Am I right? I mean, deep down, way down inside, do you believe in the world? I mean the whole world? No, you don't. And it makes you miserable to wake up with nothing to look forward to."

"Herbert," said the bartender. "You're bothering our guest."

"He wants to be bothered," Herbert said. "He loves it."

Tellerton paid for his drink and went back to Friendship's Rest. To wake up with something to look forward to—that was a phrase that instantly called up a single image of very early youth and very early morning. He went to bed, and on the verge of sleep, when everything was simplified and honest, it seemed to him that all Joe needed was to be left alone, and to be saved from disappointment for as long as possible. And all at once Bounty Joe was as distant as a children's story—just as absurd and just as legitimate.

19 Rebecca Rubinstein was writing the first draft of Abrascha's monthly letter.

"Dear Abrascha. Sometimes I toy with the idea of writing you an amusing description of the old people awaiting their final departure on the sunlit veranda of the Berkeley Arms, the most charming waiting room imaginable. But I tell myself that you can probably observe the same display of human passions, misconceptions, and lack of direction in your own surroundings, and that these weary souls can only have a purely fictional significance for you. You will never meet them. For that matter, the written word has seldom held your attention for long.

"I am sometimes fascinated by the irrational element in old age, which can add new colors to an accustomed pattern. The accumulation of past time that I see around me is heavily charged. And very malleable! I observe and I listen. I fill one of their rocking chairs and probably look like a large, slumbering walrus. But I am not asleep! I am a power station of will and insight. Give me a signal, and I operate at double strength. I can change everything if I have to. I am capable of anything if I know that I am needed."

Mrs. Rubinstein had realized a long way back that the letter could not be sent, but she went on anyway. Maybe she could use the beginning at least.

"Only now do I understand the mistakes I made and the things I left undone, but you mustn't suppose that I am regretful or apologetic. My self-confidence is undamaged, only enlarged by new vigilance. It is only now that I could . . . "

"Rebecca, dear," said Hannah Higgins, "you're not sitting on my crocheting by any chance?"

"No I'm not," said Mrs. Rubinstein. She read angrily through what she had written and crossed out everything beginning with "I am sometimes fascinated . . ." Then she lit a fresh cigarette and continued. "It's always nice to get the children's drawings. Shurele's colorful work hangs above . . . " No. ". . . the children's drawings. It sounds as if you had a pleasant Passover. Down here, we are in for more Christian entertainments in the form of an excursion to Silver Springs. The place is said to retain the beauty the Indians enjoyed before they were exterminated—with certain improvements, of course, restaurants, a snake farm, the life of Jesus in wax.

"The Spring Ball was, as usual, pathetic. And a *shlemazel* who had the unbelievable . . . " No. She didn't want to say anything about the ball. This is dreadful, thought Mrs. Rubinstein. It's like writing a paper for school. Homework for the fifteenth. An excursion. My first ball. Hah! My last ball! Poor Abrascha, do we really have to go on with this?

"I hope that Libanonna . . . " And suddenly she had forgotten what it was that Libanonna did, utterly forgotten it, which made it impossible to continue. Nothing depressed and irritated her like forgetting facts, names, words. It was absolutely impossible to concentrate on anything until the brain had recovered what it lost.

"I don't understand," said Hannah Higgins. "Where in heaven's name can I have left my crocheting?"

"Where did you last see it?" Peabody asked.

Libanonna—what was it she did? What was it that was so important? How old was she? Was she still pretty? Or maybe Shirley was the pretty one? Who knows all the things that get lost and confused and slide away when the desire to communicate is gone, and for that matter, Shirley or Libanonna or Shurele, I'll never see them anyway, those important little ladies with their great Rubinstein noses.

"Mrs. Rubinstein," said Frey. "I can see that you're sitting on Hannah's crocheting. It's sticking out behind." Mrs. Rubinstein stood up. One of the needles was bent.

"Oh, good," said Hannah Higgins, laughing. "It's a lucky thing it didn't go straight in! That would have been a pretty pickle!" Mrs. Rubinstein sat down again and closed her eyes. She thought more about Abrascha.

He was too fat even in the very first picture, the one on the white bear rug. I'll write the whole thing over. The beginning wasn't any good either. That business about the waiting room, and how he doesn't care for literature. *Narishkeit!* I'll rewrite the whole letter tomorrow.

20 The night before the big trip to Silver Springs, Joe's red motorcycle stood in front of the veranda. He had never parked right in front of the Berkeley Arms before. Now everyone could see that Joe and Linda were planning to spend the night together. Miss Ruthermer-Berkeley was glad that Linda had overcome her fear of the motorcycle, and that Bounty Joe was no longer embarrassed. In her opinion, they were saving both time and aggravation, and that could be important even when you had your whole life ahead of you. Now she must remember to convince Miss Frey. Sin, Miss Frey, sin can take on the character of pardonable irresponsibility in times of transition and change. A departure at dawn is a purely practical arrangement, for we must admit that it gets too hot later in the morning. Furthermore, an admitted transgression involves an obligation, both for them and for us. Let us hope that the responsibility they have taken upon themselves will lead to a happy marriage, and that we, on our part, will respect their boldness . . . Well, thought Miss Ruthermer-Berkeley, maybe that's getting a little long-winded. I'll have to sleep on it. But I won't ring for tea, I mustn't cause Linda any embarrassment this evening. She needs to be undisturbed.

At dawn, Joe came out onto the veranda. Under an empty sky, the city lay like a solid mass of gray—streets, houses, trees, it all looked to him like an accumulation of spider web. The only touch of life and brightness was the Honda. For the first time he saw the city's silhouette against the sky, an unfamiliar profile of spires and ornamental beauty, scrupulous and old-fashioned, like some ancient postcard from Europe. He was nervous. He realized more clearly than ever that there wasn't much time left, and that everything important was happening far away. His hands were shaking as he strapped on his helmet, and through the visor the morning turned brown as if before a storm. He waited. He felt as if he were going to be alone with Linda for the first time, and he was scared.

Finally she came, opened the gate and closed it behind her as if the welfare of the world depended on no one's being disturbed. With her helmet and her visor, and her skirt tucked into a pair of his jeans, she looked like a shapeless insect. She climbed into the saddle as if it had been a sofa, or as if she were Saint Frenesia or some other martyr ascending the stake in order to fly directly into heaven. "Sit still!" Joe whispered. "This

isn't some damned swan boat in Guadalajara." He opened the air valve on the gas tank and pulled out the
choke, checked that it was out of gear and kicked the
starter. Nothing happened—not a sound. He did it
again, nothing. He closed the choke and tried once
more. The Honda had never let him down before.
Linda sat very still and silent, but her dark insect eyes
were on him the whole time. He checked the key to be
sure the ignition was on and then kicked it again. Over
and over he hit the kick-starter as hard as he could, and
when it finally caught and exploded into life he was
weak with tension and ran it across the street and up
Friendship's sidewalk before he could get control of the
machine and bring it back into the street and drive off
in a straight line. Now she was behaving, now she was
with him. In the beginning he felt a little ill. Linda's
weight gave the Honda a new, uncertain balance. He
held the bike straight ahead and drove full out with his
chin thrust forward, feeling his own light strength in his
shoulders, his stomach, his legs. He took her up to
fourth and twisted the accelerator until it hurt his hand.
He took the curves in long, sucking arcs, sometimes in
fourth and then in third again. Linda didn't make a
sound. When the pavement was rough, it hit them like
blows in the gut. The sun came up and threw splinters
of light across the road and under the wheels, and sometimes trailer trucks would roar past in flashes of darkness
and then there was only the sun again. The unseen landscape was torn dizzyingly backward, visited by lightning
for one instant. He knew what her face looked like—the

shadows deepened by a fine layer of dust around her mouth, her hair streaming out like black smoke from underneath her helmet. She was more beautiful than ever before.

21 Johanson drove the van up in front of the house. He had decorated it with branches, a curious custom he had brought with him from Scandinavia. A blanket lay rolled up on each seat, and in the baggage space was the medicine kit, the plastic basin, and everything else they might need. Miss Frey handed out brochures. Peabody went around to the back and tried to open the rear door, but without success. She could never open anything, car doors, boxes, jars, but there was usually someone to help.

"But my dear," said Hannah Higgins, "you shouldn't sit way in the back. You'll get carsick and you won't see a thing." Peabody hesitated, then she scampered into the front seat and sat down beside Johanson.

"The mouse made her sacrifice," remarked Mrs. Rubinstein up on the veranda. "It is Christian to sit in back. If she had sat in the middle, she never could have wound up with the best place in the car. Was that an entertaining observation?"

"Well," said Elizabeth Morris. "Maybe 'nasty' is a better word."

Both of them were staying home. They didn't like excursions.

"May I go on?" Mrs. Rubinstein said. "Look at them. Elizabeth, my dear, look at them through your rose-colored glasses. Thompson is contemptuous of everything, but he's all dressed up in his black suit. They're putting him in back because he smells of garlic. Look at Frey, who hates Peabody, who hates Frey. Johanson is like Charon with his ferry, and they're off on their excursion!"

"You forgot Hannah Higgins," said Mrs. Morris.

"Elizabeth," said Mrs. Rubinstein, "I never forget Hannah Higgins, but she eludes my commentary." They were sitting in the Pihalga sisters' chairs. It seemed to be a definite decision, though unspoken.

"We're off!" called Catherine Frey. "Are you quite certain you're not staying home for our sakes?"

"Take care of yourselves!" yelled Peabody. "We're off on an adventure!" She kept waving until the car swung around the corner. Then she leaned back with a sigh, prepared to see and experience everything that came her way. Johanson drove up into town and glided into the traffic headed north and east. The highway was a solid mass of glittering cars, a long carpet of darkly gleaming metal. They entered a landscape that was like a tunnel of color. On both sides of the highway there were billboards, spires and tabernacles, glowing rainbows, letters so large that Peabody didn't have time to decipher them, rotating pillars that swelled and narrowed in a neon frenzy, hotels, motels, bungalows, all streaming toward them in an unbroken flow of beauty, enticement, and vacation.

"Florida!" cried Peabody and looked at Johanson.

"They've done a lot of building since the last time I was here," he said.

Spanish and Moroccan houses, Norwegian cabins with stones holding down their grass roofs, Japanese temples with upturned eaves! There was a gasoline station with Gothic buttresses rising toward the sky, and high in the heavens revolved an immense silver shoe. She tried to read from the top down, quickly—motel drugs stardust fiberglass we never close . . . potato chips cheap weddings—and she closed her eyes.

"Did you take your car pills?" asked Hannah Higgins behind her.

The van sank into a soft, swallowing dip and rushed under a viaduct. Parallel gratings whipped past at a ghastly speed like blinks of the eye, and the asphalt surged upward again in a widening sweep. In front of them, a shiny wash of automobiles stretched all the way to the horizon. Peabody leaned her neck against the back of the seat and watched the palm trees flash by like broomsticks. Their crowns were strangely small, just a few leaves or nothing at all, naked, pointed poles groping toward the sky. Johanson said it was from the hurricane of sixty-nine and Mrs. Higgins asked if she wanted to throw up. Peabody shook her head and swallowed, sat up straight and gazed out through the window of the car. In front of every house there were large, pink bushes, loaded down with flowers. They looked like dollops of pink pudding. Empty parking places were like missing teeth. She didn't feel well. Now the van was speeding along the ocean and white yachts came bobbing by, *Sea Belle, Tampa, Glory,* she hardly had time to read the names, *Sir Beau, Papa Lloyd . . .*. A chalk-white Christ flew past them backward, blessing the Gulf of Mexico with outstretched arms. "Johanson," she said, "Johanson, I have to get out."

Along the coast here, thoughtful authorities had built small, protected turnouts where it was possible to stop. The cars stood close together with their noses toward the billowing, green sea, and their owners stood beside them, enjoying the salt air. Evelyn Peabody threw up in the ocean.

"Feel better?" asked Hannah Higgins.

"Yes, much better. It was all happening too fast, and I wanted to see too much. It may be the only time I'll get to see Florida up close . . . " Peabody was sitting on the wall. She looked up with her vague, disarming smile. She always felt the same way after she'd been sick to her stomach—a pleasant weakness, a sort of gentle irresponsibility, like when you've been ill and get put to bed for the night. She wanted to ask Frey to forgive her.

Johanson was looking at the yachts as they glided slowly past, armed with shiny fishing tackle, strong lines, metal antennae projecting over the stern like the whiskers on a cat. The day's catch was hung in the rigging to be admired. *Papa Lloyd* had pulled in a small shark and was taking his honor lap as close to the shore as he could get. He got a round of applause wherever he went. Johanson said they were all fine boats, but of course it was easy to brag when you hadn't made anything yourself but merely paid a lot of money for it.

Maybe a cruise, thought Miss Frey, a vacation on board ship. Being carried out onto the glittering empty sea, resting in a deck chair, letting your book slip to the deck with the feeling that nothing mattered . . . She stared out over the water and was struck by the thought that that was true even now—nothing really mattered. That was what was so awful, that no matter what you did and how hard you worked and how much you gave, nothing really mattered.

Her stomach hadn't acted up for several days.

"What are you looking at?" said Peabody quietly.

"It doesn't matter," Frey said.

"The ocean's greener here than in St. Petersburg, don't you think? One time Papa took us on a long trip just to show us the ocean."

"Really," said Frey.

Peabody was still sitting on the wall. Her upturned face was oddly childlike. Groping for words, she began to explain that she was very conscious of their enmity and that in some ways she had found it very rewarding. But now all at once it seemed to her that since they were going to live together on the same veranda, why it was simpler and only right to forget their animosity.

"And be friends instead?"

"Maybe not friends, exactly," said Peabody, gazing out to sea. "There are some things you just can't decide. They either happen or they don't. What I had in mind was more of a friendly acquaintance. Life is hard enough already." Suddenly she turned toward Frey and lowered her voice. "Can you forgive me?" she said.

"By all means," said Frey. "Don't let it bother you."

Thompson got out of the car and tried to find a place where there weren't any people, but without success. So he did it anyway behind the van. He hadn't said a word on the whole trip so far.

Catherine Frey began to shiver in the sunshine. Peabody the executioner, she thought. She can say anything she wants to because of her great gentleness! She moans over an old self-sufficient scoundrel like Thompson, but to someone who's never had a friend in the world she says it's been rewarding to be enemies and now she's ready to be acquaintances! She throws up and feels better and is so affected by gazing at the ocean that she decides to ask for forgiveness—with all the cards in her hand! Frey went back to the van, where Hannah Higgins was fast asleep.

Johanson drove back out onto the highway and on toward Silver Springs. He cast an occasional glance at Thompson in the rear-view mirror, but Thompson was as distant as he had been all these past few weeks. Johanson cleared his throat and remarked that all the buildings along this stretch were new. A couple of years ago there hadn't been anything but woods.

"The things they can do!" said Miss Peabody.

By and by they began to approach the National Forest, the jungle, a pretty little part of America's untouched youth.

·   ·   ·

When the letter arrived at Palmer's with the morning mail, the bartender walked around the corner to the Berkeley Arms and asked for Linda. He didn't have time to go all the way down to the *Bounty*, he said, but he wanted to get rid of the blasted letter once and for all. Mrs. Morris was sitting on the veranda. She told him that everyone had gone to Silver Springs, that Joe and Linda had left at dawn.

"But he's got to have his letter," the bartender said.

"I know," she said. "Give it to someone at Friendship's Rest, they'll be leaving in a little while." And the bartender went across the street to where the Friendship's people were getting on their bus. He looked them over and gave the letter to Tellerton. "Now be sure Joe gets it," he said. "Bounty Joe. I couldn't care less about him or his letter, but here it is, it's come. You'll take care of it?"

"I promise," said Tellerton and put the letter in his wallet. He climbed onto the bus and it started off for Silver Springs.

"Joe," said Linda. "Oh, Joe! It's just as pretty as I thought. Springs like silver. Like being in heaven."

"How did you like the Honda?" he said.

"It was like flying into heaven!"

Joe laughed. "There, you see?" They were lying on their backs on the grass by the water. The river was as clear as glass, and where the springs swirled up little eddies formed in the steadily gliding surface. The sun was shining in the treetops, but lower down the landscape lay in shadow. Small bright red birds hopped about on the grass, scavenging among the candy bar wrappers and discarded corncobs. There was a family waiting in front of the closed ticket booth by the river boats. Four small children were eating sandwiches and drinking soda. The river boats were oval and white. They had sun roofs with fringe at the edges, and every boat had the name of an Indian chief. Linda sounded them out laboriously. "Chief Toetwo. Chief Tahatlamossee. This is where they lived," she said. "And then you took Silver Springs away from them, and killed them all." The little red birds hopped almost right up to her feet.

When the ticket booth had opened, the first river boat backed out into the current carrying only the family and Linda and Joe. They looked down into the river through glass panels set in the bottom of the boat. The sand was bathed with light, a fluttering lattice-work of bright reflections, and slim dark fish appeared and vanished in a flash, it was all so pretty! Linda lay on her face and gazed down into the water. She saw a fish with blue eyebrows, just like Mrs. Morris. And Mrs. Rubinstein sailed past with her train and veil, and Thompson swam off by himself outside the school. "Look there comes Mama, she has a little basket on her head . . . Joe! We have to swim together in the river!"

"We'll see," Joe said. He was embarrassed in front of the family.

The waterway was narrow and the jungle hung down on both sides. The trees stepped out into the river and were met in the water by tall lush plants so that the progress of the boat became a journey through an endless, green, shimmering shadowplay, a dream. "Isn't it pretty? Isn't it pretty?" Linda kept saying. She turned to the family and started talking to the children. She hugged the littlest one and laughed out loud and ran from one side of the boat to the other.

"Linda," Joe said.

"I can't help it! I'm so happy. And I'm thinking about what we are going to do before we swim in the river."

"You know there's no swimming allowed," he said.

Sometimes the boat would slow down and head in toward a tree with a white number painted on its trunk. The driver would blow a whistle and big gray monkeys would come dashing through the trees and crouch at the edge of the water to be fed. Joe bought two bags, but Linda threw badly and most of it went in the water. It didn't matter, the fish ate it up. The children shouted at the monkeys and threw their sandwich bags in the river. Suddenly a loudspeaker in the roof burst into "Ol' Man River," and the boat turned around and began to head back.

"Is it over?" Linda said. She took Joe by the shoulders and shouted, "It can't be. It has to go the whole way. Can't we go on shore and let the others go back?"

"It's not allowed," Joe said. "It's a National Forest."

"But you know what we were going to do beside the river?"

"Okay, okay," Joe said. "We'll do something later on." The family was listening. It was awful.

"Make love," Linda whispered.

He stared out across the river.

When they got ashore, Bounty Joe threw himself down on his stomach in the grass and wouldn't say anything. Linda lay down right beside him. "You're angry," she said. "You think I have disgraced you. You are so strange in this country. Everything you sing and write and your pictures and your clothes and your Jesus is all about love. You dance like you were making love. But no one may talk about it."

"It was that family," Joe said. "They were listening."

"Families," said Linda patiently. "Families know all about love, Joe. If Mama wanted to love Papa she said now we have time and here is a good spot. We all heard what she said. And she was right, because Papa always wanted to."

"You talk too much," Joe said.

The bus from Friendship's Rest drove up in front of the restaurant. He saw them getting off one by one, and all of them stood and stared at the river. And all at once, like a sudden wind, Joe wanted to possess Linda, here, now, in the grass by the water, and he rolled over on his back and gazed at the tops of the trees.

When Hannah Higgins arrived at Silver Springs, she clapped her hands in delight. "It's just like a picture book!" she cried.

Here everyone could walk on the grass. Families, tourists, loving couples, old people, children, everyone. They strolled around, they played and dreamed, they ate and slept on the grass. The boats sailed up and down the river for all they were worth, each of them named for an Indian chief. They had lived here a long time ago, hunted and swum and cooked their food. It was strange to think about. The same springs and the same fish, but of course now the whole thing was protected.

"Just like a pretty picture book," said Hannah Higgins again as she went into the souvenir shop. She bought some postcards and three little Indians to send home. Peabody found a scarf with all the sights of Silver Springs, but Frey just stood and leafed through her brochures. Her stomach was acting up again. "Where is Thompson?" she said. "I'm responsible for this trip, and we have to keep together." Hannah Higgins replied that he had bought himself a Davy Crockett cap. The new cap was big and gray and had a long tail. Along with his eyebrows, it made Thompson look almost diabolical. And at the same time it seemed to make him smaller.

"Won't it be too hot?" Peabody wondered.

Not for him, thought Frey. Not where he's from! "The first thing on our program is the snake farm," she said. "You can all go in if you want to, but I'll wait outside. It makes me sick just to look at anything that crawls."

"Freudian," Thompson said. It was the first time he had said anything. The new cap had cheered him up. He glowered at Frey from under his fur brim, shook his gray tail, and went into the snake house. It was already very warm. The three travelers walked from window to window and gazed at motionless, coiled snakes. Most of them looked dusty and appeared to be asleep. Thompson pressed his face against the glass and made terrible faces to try to get the snakes to move. "They're just like me," he said. "They despise the whole world."

Mrs. Higgins and Miss Peabody started talking about snakes. They told each other dreadful stories about swimming snakes that crawled up on a person in the water and white snakes that came to the steps when someone was going to die . . . Snakes that grabbed their own tails and chased people like hoops!

"Talk louder!" Thompson said. "I can't hear what you're saying."

Hannah Higgins repeated it. "In South America they bite their own tails and come rolling after you like a hoop! And one time when we were making hay, a snake got caught on my pitchfork and crawled right down across my throat!"

Evelyn Peabody shrieked, a little mouse cry.

"Snakes," said Thompson. "Snakes, my dear ladies, you've got snakes on the brain. Poor animals. You can't get over the Garden of Eden, can you?" He had a sudden euphoric desire to talk. He pulled the fur cap farther down over his eyes and hissed, "Snakes! Sex! You've got them on the brain, and you can't get rid of them. I can tell you all that snake wants is to be left in peace. He would never chase you like a hoop, not even in South America! Look at him! Have you ever seen such an utter lack of interest? Such vast contempt?" A cobra lifted its slowly swaying, hooded head. It had the eyes of a bird of prey or a crocodile. Then it moved its head backward a hair's breadth and stiffened. "Come away, come away," Miss Peabody whispered. They walked on across the hot sand.

The snake trainer stood in his cage surrounded by eight rattlesnakes. He was wearing high boots. Three busloads of people encircled his shatterproof glass square. The snakes lay around him in a circle, tightly coiled, and in the middle of each coil was a steady warning rattle. The sound was dry and lifeless and full of ice-cold menace.

"Come over here," said Hannah Higgins. "We can see better."

Tim Tellerton was standing across from them on the other side. The bus from Friendship's had arrived. The snake trainer raised his arm and the eight sets of rattles increased their tempo, matter-of-factly promising death. Tellerton looked at them with controlled distaste and hoped that they would not uncoil. The snake trainer blew up a white balloon. Slowly, dramatically, he extended the balloon toward one of the snakes, closer and closer. No one could see the snake strike—not even the shadow of a movement. There was only a faint bang, a plastic rag, and a shudder of satisfaction around the shatterproof cage. Thompson elbowed his way around to the other side and tapped Tellerton on the shoulder. "I remember you," he said. "You didn't want to sit in the dead ladies' rocking chairs. Do you feel sorry for snakes?"

Tellerton looked at the snakes and said, "Yes, I feel sorry for them."

"That's what I thought," Thompson said and went away.

The snake trainer got a nice hand and then left the

cage. The people outside the glass began slowly wandering away. The snakes stayed tightly coiled, and their rattles continued to sound.

A new busload of people approached across the sand, and the rattlers remained in battle-readiness all day.

"Miss Peabody," said Tellerton. "Have you seen Bounty Joe?" The question was formal and impersonal, like a question asked at a box office or a counter.

"No," she said.

"I have an important letter for him, a letter that came to Palmer's this morning." They were swept up by the crowd of people moving toward the alligator tank.

"How do you like St. Petersburg?" Evelyn Peabody asked.

"Beg pardon?" said Tellerton.

"How do you like St. Petersburg?"

"It's a very lovely city."

The animals lay in a pile in one corner of the tank, dry, rough bodies in a petrified heap. A water faucet was dripping on them. The crowd was pressing forward. Peabody asked him with hostility in her voice if they had given him a pleasant room. He looked at her in bewilderment. "A room," he said. "Yes, a very nice room. Shall we move along?"

It was hard to escape the crowd, which was milling aimlessly. People were getting in each other's way, not knowing where they wanted to go or what they wanted to see. Several more busses had arrived. Old people mostly, they walked too slowly and went in the wrong direction. There was always the same problem fitting them into the flow of normal traffic. "Move along here," said the guard. "Do you want to go out, or do you want to go in?"

"Mr. Tellerton," said Peabody. "I've seen you on the stage." People were pressing in on them from every side. He glanced around now and then to see if she was still behind him. "On the stage!" she shouted. "It meant a great deal to me!"

They were pushed past the ticket booth, and Miss Frey ran up to them and said so there they were, at last. She had bought them all tickets for a trip on the river.

"Wait, wait," said Peabody. She looked at Tellerton.

"Please," he said. "If you see Bounty Joe, tell him his letter came."

The river boat was full. They were each given a bag of food for the fish. The loudspeaker came on, and they glided out onto the shimmering river.

It was a long, full day. Those who got tired could rest on the terraces or in the shade of the trees. Those with more stamina strolled along the green banks of some waterway. The little children tumbled on the grass or slept on their backs with their arms over their heads, as open as flowers. Young people shot at targets with long, feathered arrows. When Hannah Higgins passed the archery range with its huge enlargement of Chief Tahatlamossee, she heard the ringing tones of the bows and stopped to look. She could see bright colored Indian designs inside the fence, and far away the targets shone like suns. Behind them was the dense wall of the jungle.

"Couldn't we go in?" said Mrs. Higgins. "It's only

twenty-five cents, and I've never seen anyone shoot a bow and arrow." Miss Frey said they didn't have time. They had Bambi's Playground on the program, and then they had to go home.

"Wait a little," said Mrs. Higgins and went closer. "Just a little while." Thanks to her poor eyes, colors always flowed out over their borders and mixed with the light very luminously. No one knew that Hannah Higgins saw the world much prettier than it was. Not only colors but movements too were intensified. In her eyes, all movement underwent an expressive simplification. Where the young Hannah had seen what she was used to seeing, the old Hannah saw reality freed from habit and unnecessary detail. The essential part of a color or a movement was always strongest toward the end of the day. The archers were wonderfully beautiful, slim and straight. She saw their bodies bend the way bows are bent, calmly and dramatically. And they were just as pretty when they lowered the bows in a gesture of attentive relaxation.

Frey repeated that it was late. She had tickets for Bambi's Playground, and small animals grew tired just before the sun went down. She wanted Evelyn and Thompson to see the Playground before the animals went to sleep.

"That's so true," said Mrs. Higgins. "I think I'll take a little nap myself in Johanson's van."

He was sitting on the terrace with his newspaper.

"Johanson," said Mrs. Higgins, "here's twenty-five cents. I want you to go shoot an arrow for me, as far as you can. You can shoot a bow and arrow, can't you?"

"Of course I can," he said.

"Of course he can!" Thompson shouted. "Grandpa Johanson can do anything in the world, I'll bet. But he doesn't know a thing about jungles! He'll shoot one of my tigers. I'm very attached to the tigers and the snakes and the Indian chiefs!"

"Don't worry," Johanson said. "I'll shoot in the air. Mr. Thompson needn't worry about the tigers."

Miss Frey led them on toward the Playground.

"What an ass," said Thompson. "If he thinks there are tigers at Silver Springs, then he's dumber than I thought."

Right up against the wall of the jungle and encircled by a palisade, Bambi's Playground was at a constant greenhouse temperature. Here all the animals were tame and didn't bite. Anyone who wanted to could buy baby bottles full of warm milk and feed the fawns or hold the rabbits and the kittens on their lap. There were goats everywhere, bleating and jostling. They would draw their long gray lips up over their teeth and try to chew at people's clothes. Pigeons would light on shoulders and hands in perfect trust. Children would get frightened and scream and be comforted and photographed embracing feeding animals. Over this incredibly friendly and gentle throng hung the odor of children, warm sand, boiled milk, and urine.

Tim Tellerton stopped in the entrance. He stood still and searched among the people for Bounty Joe.

"Oh my heavens, the letter!" cried Peabody. "They were here a little while ago and I forgot to tell them about the letter. Linda was giving milk to a Bambi and I just forgot!"

Tellerton smiled wanly. She shouldn't worry about it. There was plenty of time. He looked very tired. Beside them, someone had put a coin in the rabbit machine, the trap door fell open and two rabbits rushed out from opposite sides, started the roulette with their front paws, and rolled it hysterically. The machine gave a clang and stopped on white. A thin stream of oats spilled onto the floor of the cage.

Evelyn Peabody had been standing there looking at Tellerton and for the first time she could see that he was a very old man, a perfectly ordinary old man with beautiful eyes. Poor soul, she thought automatically, he must be tired, and her compassion returned to accustomed paths that she knew and was used to and that were not cramped by admiration. She stepped closer and said there were benches in the playhouse, maybe he would like to rest. Tim Tellerton turned his eyes on her, as cold as ice. "Miss Peabody," he said. "You are much too kind."

Just then Catherine Frey started screaming at the tame pigeons. She waved her arms and chased the birds as young animals stumbled out of her way bleating helplessly and children turned around in fear. The guard rushed forward. "Listen here," he said. "This is a nursery, we can't have disturbances in here!" Frey turned her back and searched through her purse with trembling hands.

"It's just nerves," Peabody told the guard in a whisper. "I'll take care of it and get her calmed down."

Frey walked away from them. You little ministering angel you, she thought, and wandered blindly in under the overhanging jungle and stopped at the palisade. There was a white gate with a sign that said JUNGLE TRAIL. The goats had followed her and were trying to get at her hands.

"Miss Frey," said Tim Tellerton. "Might I ask you a favor? I know I can count on you."

"Of course," she said. "What can I do for you?" And she pressed her hands together to keep them from trembling.

"I have a letter for Bounty Joe," said Tellerton gravely. "It's an important letter that arrived at Palmer's this morning. Can you see that he gets it?"

"Yes. Yes, of course," said Frey. She took the letter and put it in her purse. The goats began to nibble at the purse and she lifted it out of reach. They were pushing at her from all sides. They smelled foul.

"Miss Frey," said Tellerton, "I feel like a stranger here, and I appreciate your help. Please convey my greetings to the Berkeley Arms." He held the white gate for her, and with a quick, professional bow he left the Playground.

Catherine Frey found herself on the Jungle Trail. The Jungle Trail was included in the price. It wasn't long, only ten minutes out and back, but the visitor did get a strong impression of genuine jungle. And after the busses had stopped arriving, late on a weekday, the trail seemed empty and the forest absolutely silent.

She stood perfectly still for quite some time. The sunshine was gone, and there were no animals. It was pleasant. By and by she walked on. The ground was damp, but the path was of corduroy logs and enclosed with ropes. Beyond the ropes lay the jungle, dense and low, mangrove trees with water between their roots and gray heaps of swollen moss like burial mounds. Peabody, the cruel angel of compassion right up to the day she died. Here lies Evelyn Peabody of the tender heart. Here lies the colorful Mr. Thompson. Here lies Frey. The music from the river boats reached her very faintly, and then she heard the others, Peabody and Thompson coming after her. "Wait!" called Peabody. "How are you feeling? Are you better? How are your nerves?" Thompson sniffed around and declared that this was no jungle at all, it was nothing like a jungle. He went over to the rope and stared into a gray thicket. He was very disappointed. His own jungle was dark green and impenetrable. His trees were frightening in their immensity and rose out of perpetual dusk toward an inaccessible roof of orchids, a flaming jungle roof over wild animals, dreamers, and mad millionaires. Ha! This was a promenade for little old ladies!

"This is an absolutely genuine jungle," Peabody declared. "It's a National Forest. No one has set foot in there for decades, or broken a twig. They say farther in there are wild monkeys. Wait a minute." She took out her brochure and began to leaf through it.

"Peabody," said Thompson, "you talk like a guide. Without beer you have no imagination." He walked on at a limping trot with his cane beating on the corduroy and populated his jungle with things that crawled and crept, heavy bodies that scurried through the thickets as

204 · TOVE JANSSON

silently as silk, a leap torn into rasping pieces and a scream cut off abruptly, hardly a gasp. "Snakes," he said over his shoulder. "I like them. I had a viper that slept under my bed."

Catherine Frey passed him and started walking faster. Thompson raised his voice. "A viper! And how do you know I don't still have one under my bed? A big black viper! You'll never find it, but you'll never be sure it isn't around the house someplace."

Frey swung around. "What is it you want?" she said. "Why do you do everything you can think of to frighten and annoy me? Why do you do that?"

"To see if it'll work," said Thompson from under the brim of his cap. It seemed to be a perfectly honest answer.

"Don't be mean!" cried Peabody anxiously. "She doesn't like animals."

Catherine Frey walked away from them. Pretty soon she came to the clearing in the forest where the path turned around and went back. A sign announced that this was the JUNGLE CLEARING, and a little South Pacific pavilion offered a place to rest. She went in and sat down. Aspirin didn't usually help, but she took a couple anyway. There were machines selling sandwiches, postcards, and Coca-Cola. In the middle of the clearing stood a red and white plywood Santa Claus with snow on his back, surrounded by huge toadstools. The inevitable totem pole gazed insanely into the jungle. She relaxed a little—maybe the aspirin was helping after all. Catherine Frey let herself drift into unreality and a sense of being completely overwhelmed, and the scenery and the people around her seemed exaggerated, like cartoons, and she was merely tired.

Then Peabody and Thompson arrived. Peabody looked into one of the hollow toadstools and said they ought to make a wish, as long as they were here. You just wrote it down and put it in and you could wish for anything at all, and did Frey have a little piece of paper?

Make a wish for me, thought Catherine Frey. Wish three times that I was dead. And put in some mignonette and a little rosemary, and while you're at it, stuff in as much of your papa as there's room for, and for Jesus' sake leave me in peace.

"Why are you laughing?" Peabody said. "Don't you have any paper?" Just then Thompson lifted the rope around the clearing and walked off into the jungle. His gray fur cap disappeared among the trees.

"No, I don't have any paper," Frey said.

Peabody came in and sat down in the pavilion. The silence frightened her, so she launched into a long discourse that seemed to deal mostly with how strange it was that people didn't always mean what they said or say what they meant, and how a person mustn't let things get her down, because they so seldom turned out the way you thought, and most people really meant well . . . She had an uneasy feeling of having been unfriendly. A trace of conscience had begun to gnaw at her again, though it wasn't yet localized.

"Where is he?" Frey asked suddenly.

"Thompson? I think he went in the jungle."

"Did you see him go into the jungle?"

"I don't know. I don't know for sure . . ."

"Did you see him? Did you?" Frey burst out. "Don't fib. Tell me if you saw him!"

"Maybe he did," Evelyn Peabody whispered.

Miss Frey leaped up and ran out into the clearing. She shouted for Thompson over and over again, but there was no answer. He must have heard her, he couldn't have gone far, but the old goat didn't answer. He was stone deaf today and had escaped from the sandbox. She lifted the rope and went after him.

"Wait!" screamed Peabody. "Wait for me!"

Catherine Frey walked on, moved by her responsibility but maybe even more so by her anger. Now and then she called her enemy. The ground became soft, a dark, indefinite mass that her feet sank into. It was hard to walk. The water in her shoes was warm. The rotting trunks of mangrove trees stuck up everywhere. They were smaller at the top, like angle worms. It was a hideous forest. Finally she started shouting just to shout, to scream off her rage. "You old goat! Pyromaniac! Thompson! You foul man!" And as she walked, deeper and deeper into the jungle, she began to scream at the others too. Terrible epithets aimed at the people who had never taken the trouble to ask, never bothered to look for the one person in the world who was Catherine Frey.

Peabody followed as well as she could. She heard Frey shouting farther and farther away in the forest, more and more faintly. At last it was silent.

There was nothing so frightening as to have people leave you behind and not bother to wait. It felt awful even when she was little and the whole thing was only a game. No one knew how it scared her every time Papa wanted to play. Every time he hid behind a tree she thought he would never come back. Every time he failed to find what he was looking for, his daughter Evelyn was plunged in sorrow. We searched, we never did anything but search. He couldn't find the spring for us, and not the jungle either. My dear little family, suppose that here we have a genuine mangrove swamp. Imagine black reflections under curiously shaped roots and the smell of stagnant water seething with putrefaction . . . All sorts of dangers surround us. Comfort your mother! I'll find a place for all of you, a place that is safe and dry. Oh George, said Mama, stop. And I prayed to God that he would find his mangrove swamp and the safe place that Mama would admire, and all the time I was afraid that he would get tired and die because we always let him be disappointed. And I was absolutely right, thought Miss Peabody. That was exactly what he did, young as he was. She stumbled into a mudhole and her glasses flew off. While searching for them, she trampled them into the moss.

The jungle was a world of water. Every time Linda found a pretty spot for making love, the ground would sink away into deep, brown water. "You see how it is," Joe said. "And why do you have to have flowers? They'll just get flattened if we lie on them, and they won't show anyway." "Yes," said Linda and waded on between mangrove islands, peering about like a water bird. When branches blocked their way, she bent them aside and waited for Joe to step by, and then she led the way

again. It was already late in the afternoon, and the forest
lay in shadow. "Here," she said. "Here we won't sink so
deep—we can make love in the water." But Joe said
they'd have to be eels to make it work, and he didn't
like to feel ridiculous. Linda didn't answer. Finally they
came to a place where there was a current coiling in
among the trees and the dark surface was covered with
flocks of water lilies and round, green lily pads. "Here,"
she said. "We couldn't find a better place to swim. And
it's almost as much fun just to swim." They took off
their clothes and hung them on a tree. Near the shore
was a tangle of sunken roots, but out in the middle
there was a solid sand bottom. Joe looked at Linda. The
lily pads had gathered a wreath around her waist, and
she pushed them aside and let herself glide into the
water. She looked at him but didn't think of love. They
floated in the gentle current with their faces toward the
sky, and it was like sailing in the air. "If you're hungry,"
she said, "and want a hamburger or something we still
have time to get to the restaurant before they close."

"I'm not hungry," Joe said. "This is nice."

The water at Silver Springs was as pure as the ocean
in Miami. Maybe purer.

Catherine Frey walked on into the National Forest, quietly now, without shouting. Her stomach had stopped
hurting. No thoughts pursued her. The last river boat
had turned and sailed back to Silver Springs and the
loudspeakers were all turned off and pretty soon the
gates would close. She walked on. Some gray monkeys
sat hunched up in the trees. They looked like Thomp-

son in his coonskin cap. The whole forest was gray and unreal, the mangroves and the water holes and the swollen earth she walked on without caring about a thing except that her stomach had stopped hurting. It was like falling asleep and leaving everything behind and walking further and further into a calm and indifferent emptiness.

Miss Frey was not herself. She had overstepped the bounds of her own exhausted sobriety. Perhaps she was lured on by some dark vision of ancient elephants walking straight into their innermost wilderness to be left in peace—that was possible.

Afterward, Miss Frey thought she had been lost, but sometimes even then she would secretly indulge a wonder and a daydream that had to do with the beauty of emptiness and extinction.

Since Miss Frey, like most people, took slightly longer steps with her right leg than with her left, she moved in a large circle that eventually brought her back toward Silver Springs. Just before sunset she stopped by a small waterway, hardly more than a passage for turtles and fish. Indescribably untouched, the stream ran by under its roof of broad, gleaming leaves, and suddenly, like a natural part of the spring, two swimmers came gliding along in the current. They did not take long to float by. They didn't raise a shoulder above the surface. Joe was the brown color of the spring itself, and Linda was as white as the sand. Her hair spread out in the current like a broad, finely penciled shadow.

When they were gone, the emptiness of the forest was changed.

Frey began to cry laboriously. She sat down on a tree trunk and took her handkerchief out of her purse. She glanced at her watch and saw that it was late and that Johanson should have started home long ago. They had a long trip in front of them. Miss Frey tidied up her purse, putting the receipts for the day's entertainments in one pocket and the brochures in another. She put her change in her coin purse and stuffed the damp handkerchief in her pocket so that Joe's letter would not get wet. Finally she powdered her nose and stood up to walk back, but she didn't move and had no idea which way to go.

Just then, at sunset, the archers assembled for the big match of the day. Every day the prize was the same, a medal with a likeness in relief of the Indian Chief Tahatlamossee, who in merciless savagery had defended Silver Springs to the bitter end. He was still there in wax, in an authentic copy of the prison where he had died of a broken heart. When Miss Frey looked up toward the sky, she saw an arrow rising steeply in the air, strongly lit by the setting sun. It had red and white feathers. For one long, restful moment, the arrow seemed to pause before it fell, very fast, straight down into the jungle. Miss Frey put her purse under her arm and started walking toward Silver Springs in a straight line. Pretty soon she saw Peabody standing with her arms around a tree. "Hello," said Frey. "Have you seen Thompson? We have to get back, it's late." Peabody just shook her head and didn't move.

"Don't get excited," said Frey. "It's late. I'll have to talk to the office and get them to look for him right away, or else we won't get home until the middle of the night."

"It was your fault," Peabody whispered. "You wouldn't wait, and you went away and I dropped them in the moss." She raised her voice. "I saw it happen," she wailed. "He died and sank under the water!"

"Now calm down and let go of that tree. What are you talking about?"

"He sank under the water!" Peabody screamed. "I saw him float by, he was big and tall!"

"Thompson? Are you talking about Thompson?"

"No! I'm talking about him! He sank, he ran out of strength and just disappeared."

"Listen to me," said Frey, getting scared. She took Peabody by the shoulders and spoke to her carefully. "What did you see? Think! Did you see the arrow falling? They shot an arrow from Silver Springs, did you see it? Don't fib. Do you know what you're saying?"

"Of course I know!" Peabody shouted, growing angry. "He died too young, but old biddies like you just go on and on and can't take care of anything, even though you're in charge of the whole program."

"Give me your arm," Frey said. "We're going home." They walked slowly toward the park. The totem pole emerged from among the trees, white and black with its gaping mouths, and the Santa Claus with his toadstools. Nothing had changed. "Are you mad at me?" Peabody asked. "Say something. Do you think I'll get a cold from this?"

"You might," Frey said. "It's possible. Put on some dry socks in the car."

Peabody hung heavily on her shoulder and stumbled constantly. Peabody had grown old, and you couldn't be angry with her. Her eyes and her thoughts both sharp, Miss Frey walked down the Jungle Trail. She was not tired. She was the bearer of evil news. For many years to come they would sit on the veranda in St. Petersburg and talk about Joe, over and over again, the handsome boy, the vast jungle, one single Joe and one single arrow and hundreds of miles of empty and untrodden forest, oh God it was so awful and so strange.

"Do you think we'll be in time?" Peabody said. "Are we going to be late?"

"Take it easy," Frey said. "We have plenty of time. It's not dark yet, not nearly."

When the telephone rang in the vestibule, Mrs. Rubinstein had written the address on Abrascha's letter and lay reading in bed. She counted six rings before it stopped. After a while it started again, six rings and then silence. "Ha!" said Rebecca Rubinstein. "They call and disturb you in the middle of the night." She couldn't go on reading. An anxiety had been kindled and quickly grew, as terrible as in those long forgotten nights when Abrascha hadn't yet come home, and now they were calling again. She threw off the quilt and stumbled out to the stairs. It was dark. Elizabeth Morris answered the phone downstairs. She said very little. In a few moments the phone would be hung up and steps would slowly mount the stairs searching for gentle words—You must be brave, your son . . .

Rebecca Rubinstein leaned against the railing and

waited. A new letter sprang forth, the letter she could have written and had always tried to write, simple, without a single word that disguised or concealed, and while she spoke to him in terrible haste and finally, without searching, found the cooling love they had needed and missed for so long, while she wrote page after page, Elizabeth Morris came back and started slowly up the stairs and said, "Don't turn on the light, I don't have my teeth in. That was Johanson. They've been delayed and won't be back until later tonight. Thompson has made some sort of trouble and Frey is very ill . . . "

"What are you saying?" whispered Mrs. Rubinstein. "Is that all? Isn't there something else?"

"Yes," said Mrs. Morris. "I talked to Linda. Joe got his letter from Miami. He's leaving tomorrow, as soon as he can." She paused for a moment. "They're in a bad way," she said. "Thompson is completely out of hand and insists that Johanson has shot one of his monkeys . . ."

"One of his monkeys," said Mrs. Rubinstein. She wanted to shout, to laugh, to sing, and her legs began to shake and she held onto the railing with both hands.

"What's the matter with you?" Elizabeth said.

"Nothing, you must forgive me, I have a letter to write." She was impatient. "I know their excursion was difficult. It had to be. Elizabeth, I don't have time to worry about it. Grandpa Johanson has shot a monkey, and that's too bad, but it's late. If I don't write that letter now I never will."

"I understand," said Mrs. Morris. She went back to her bed.

Sleep is a blessing that a person can meet in many different ways. Tonight Mrs. Morris slept very lightly, the way a person sleeps before an important departure—with complete attention. Sometime between one and two she got up, put in her teeth, and dressed carefully. When she had turned on the lights on the stairs and in the vestibule and on the veranda, she turned on the lights in Linda's room. Then Mrs. Morris went out in the warm night and sat in Pihalga's rocking chair. It was cloudy, and the Berkeley Arms was lit like a palace awaiting belated guests.

OTHER NEW YORK REVIEW CLASSICS

For a complete list of titles, visit www.nyrb.com.